Jack McCall got up off his cot and came over to the front of the cell. Pushing his face against the bars he asked, "Who is that guy, anyway?"

"A friend of the man you killed," Marshal Hanks answered.

"What's his name?"

"If I tell you you're just gonna lose sleep worrying about it," Hanks said.

"Damn it—" McCall cursed.

"All right, McCall, I warned you. His name is Clint Adams, some people call him the Gunsmith."

McCall's eyes popped.

"See?" Hanks said. "I warned you. Pleasant dreams!"

Don't miss any of the lusty, hard-riding action in the
new Charter Western series, THE GUNSMITH:

And coming next month:

THE GUNSMITH #15: BANDIT GOLD

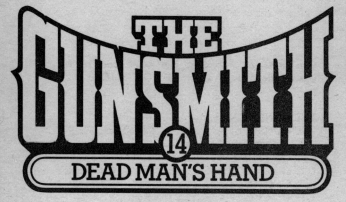

THE GUNSMITH

14

DEAD MAN'S HAND

J.R. ROBERTS

CHARTER BOOKS, NEW YORK

All characters in this book are fictitious.
Any resemblance to actual persons, living or dead,
is purely coincidental.

THE GUNSMITH #14: DEAD MAN'S HAND
A Charter Book / published by arrangement with
the author

PRINTING HISTORY
Charter edition / March 1983

ISBN: 0-441-30869-4

Charter Books are published by Charter Communications, Inc.
200 Madison Avenue, New York, New York 10016.
PRINTED IN THE UNITED STATES OF AMERICA

Dedication

To Anna,
Happy Birthday

DEAD MAN'S HAND

ONE

Clint Adams, the Gunsmith, was in Texas when he heard the news of the death of his greatest friend, James Butler "Wild Bill" Hickok. Hickok did not just *die,* however; he was killed, shot from behind while playing poker in a saloon in Deadwood Gulch, Dakota Territory.

The death of Wild Bill hit Clint Adams hard, harder than he had ever been hit before, but only part of it was the death of his best friend. The other part was the way Hickok had been killed.

How could Bill have allowed himself to be caught that way? For years he had made it a practice to sit with his back to the wall, and for even more years, the Gunsmith had lived by the same practice.

Now Bill was dead.

Clint Adams feared one thing in his life, and that

was having it come to an end as the result of a coward's bullet in the back.

The way Bill Hickok's life had ended, on August 2, 1876.

"Another bottle," Clint told the bartender.

"Don't you think you've had enough, Mr. Adams?" the young bartender asked, eyeing the Gunsmith warily.

"After two weeks, how much is enough?" another voice asked. It was Rick, the owner of the saloon. "Give him another bottle, T.C.," he instructed the bartender.

"Whatever you say, boss."

Clint took the bottle from the bartender and then lurched to a corner table with it, where he sat himself down against the wall with his back pressed firmly up against it.

"That guy ain't gonna last much longer," T.C. said.

"He took it hard," Rick said.

'Hickok?"

"Yeah."

"That's tough."

"Yeah. Give me a glass, will you?"

Rick Hartman took the empty glass and walked over to Clint Adams's table.

"Mind if I sit down?"

"It's your saloon."

The Gunsmith had been in the town of Labyrinth, Texas for a week before hearing the news about Hickok's death. During that time, he had become fairly friendly with Rick Hartman. Hartman felt that this entitled him to stick his nose in Clint's business.

"Mind?" Hartman asked, indicating the whiskey bottle.

"It's your place," Clint replied again.

Hartman poured himself a shot then sat back in his chair and took a look at Clint Adams. He hadn't shaved in two weeks, and Hartman doubted that he had bathed either. He'd spent most of his waking hours—and some of his sleeping ones—right there at that table, and Hartman wanted to get him out for his own good before he took root.

"Clint, don't you think it's about time you got yourself cleaned up?"

"What for?"

"For your own good, man," Hartman answered. "This isn't getting you anywhere. I mean, I know you lost a friend, but—"

"A friend," Clint repeated, staring at the saloon owner through bloodshot eyes. "Bill Hickok was more than a friend, Hartman."

"All right," Hartman said. "All I'm saying is that it isn't going to do him or you any good if you kill yourself."

Hartman watched as Clint poured himself another drink and pointedly ignored him. When he reached for the bottle, the Gunsmith's brown eyes pinned him with an ice-cold stare.

"I'm cutting you off, Clint," Hartman told him.

"You mean you're going to try."

"What are you gonna do, draw on me?" Hartman asked. "I don't think you could hit me from where you're sitting. Look at your hands, friend."

Clint stuck his hands out in front of him, and there was a highly perceptible shake to each one.

"You might even drop the gun trying to get it out of your holster," Hartman said, taking the bottle.

Clint put his hands flat down on the table and pushed himself unsteadily to his feet.

"There are other places to drink."

"Sure," Hartman said. "Drink all you want, Clint. Set yourself up to be taken by some second-rate gun-hawk who won't care how drunk you are or how much your hands are shaking when he kills you. All he'll care about is that he gunned down the Gunsmith— and not the way Hickok got it. He'll take you from the front, and you won't be able to do anything about it!"

"You're crazy," Clint said. He pushed the table out so that he could move around it and headed for the batwing doors.

"I tried," Hartman said to no one in particular. "I really tried." He looked at the bottle in his hand, then poured himself a drink from it and silently toasted the memory of Bill Hickok.

He sincerely hoped that he wouldn't also be toasting the memory of the Gunsmith in the near future.

It was almost the end of August when Rick Hartman decided that he should try once more to drag Clint Adams out of the gutter. He thought that the article he had just read in the papers just might do the trick.

He got up from his table and walked to the bar.

"T.C., where is Adams doing his drinking these days?"

"Since you cut him off, I heard he's been hanging out at the Blue Garter Saloon."

"Over the red line?" Hartman asked.

"That's what I hear, boss."

Many towns in the West had what they called the "red line"—the border between the decent part of town and the . . . less-than-decent part of town. Over the red line a man had a fairly good chance of losing his poke—or his life—simply by walking down the street—and that was in broad daylight!

Hartman decided that a chance at saving Clint Adams from a life in the bottle—or a death because of it—was worth the risk.

Folding the newspaper, he stuffed it into his jacket pocket and left to find Clint Adams.

Hartman was no stranger to the red line, and a few people in that section greeted the tall, well-built man as he walked down the street. The truth of the matter was, Rick Hartman started in that part of town and worked his way up to Rick's Place. He never thought anything would be able to get him back to that part of town willingly, but here he was, mounting the boardwalk in front of the Blue Garter, which he himself had started some years ago.

Inside, the place looked even worse than he remembered, but there could be no denying that it was a moneymaker. The Garter was packed, and a goodly portion of the people had to be paying customers.

"Well, well, look who's here," a voice called above the din. "Slumming, Hartman, or you want to buy the place back?"

The speaker was John Denson, a tall, slim man about Hartman's own age—forty, or so—who, like Hartman, was somewhat overdressed for his surroundings.

"Hello, Denson," Hartman said. The two men weren't friends, but neither were they enemies. They respected each other and treated each other accordingly.

"What brings you back to this part of town?" Denson asked.

"I'm looking for someone, John."

"Oh? Who?"

"Clint Adams."

"Ah, the ex-Gunsmith."

"What do you mean by that?"

Denson shrugged. "I've seen men fall into a bottle before, Rick. So have you. He's getting in so deep he'll never be able to get out. His days as a gun are— well, numbered, at best." Denson shook his head and said, "It's a damn shame, too, to have to lose two legends in one month."

"We're not going to lose him if I can help it," Hartman said. "Where is he?"

"Maybe he's lucky you're here," Denson said. "There've been a few guys watching him all night. I think they're waiting for a chance to—uh-oh."

"What?"

Denson was looking at an empty table, and then he pointed to another one.

"He was sitting at one of those tables, and the others were sitting at the other one. They're all gone now."

"How long ago?"

"Couldn't be more than a minute or two," Denson said. "I was watching him, and then I saw you come in."

Hartman looked around, then remembered the back room, which led out to an alleyway.

"The back," he said, and rushed through the crowd to the door in the back of the room. He was dimly aware of people shouting and of Denson, who was on his heels. When he reached the door he threw it open and rushed through. The Colt Cloverleaf that had been in his shoulder holster was now in his hand.

"Empty," Denson said, behind him.

"Outside," Hartman said, and they darted across to the back door.

As they ran into the back alley, they could see what was going on very clearly in the moonlight. Three men were pummeling Adams, who was on the ground with both hands attempting to cover his head. He was making no effort to fight back, or to go for his gun.

"Gunsmith, my ass," one of the men was saying. "He ain't shit."

"Hold it," Hartman shouted, and all three men turned in the direction of his voice.

"Get 'em!" one of them yelled, and they all went for their guns.

Hartman fired one shot from his Cloverleaf, catching one of the men in the chest. Denson had his S&W Pocket .38 out, and he fired, striking another man in the throat. The third man, aware that he was now outnumbered, tried to turn and run, but both Denson and Hartman fired, and both slugs struck the fleeing man in the back.

"How many were there inside?" Hartman asked Denson.

"Three," Denson answered.

"Cover me," Hartman said. "There may have been someone waiting out here for them."

"Right."

Hartman put away his gun, while Denson kept his out, to cover both Hartman and Clint.

Hartman went over to Clint, who hadn't moved, and grabbed him beneath the arms.

"Come on, damn it. Get up!" he snapped, pulling Clint to his feet.

"I need a drink," Clint muttered. "A drink."

"Yeah, you need a drink," Hartman said. "Let's go inside."

Supporting Clint, Hartman walked him past Denson and into the back room of the saloon. Denson, still holding his gun, backed in after them and shut the door.

The door leading to the saloon opened and a man came running in. Denson turned, training his gun on the man, but when he saw who it was, he lowered it.

"Hog," he said.

Hog looked at his boss and said, "I heard shots. What happened?"

"Get the sheriff, Hog," Denson said. "We'll tell him and you at the same time."

The big man nodded and went for the sheriff.

"I need a drink," Clint Adams said, louder than before.

"Yeah," Hartman said, again, "you need a drink. John, can we get some light in here?"

"Sure," Denson said. He lit a lamp, then went over to stand next to Hartman, who had taken a newspaper out of his pocket.

"What's that?" he asked.

"You'll see."

Clint was sitting on the floor, holding his head in his hands.

"Clint, I want you to read something. Can you read something?" Hartman asked him.

Shaking his head Clint said, "I don't want to read. I want a drink."

"First you read something," Hartman said. "Then if you want a drink I'll get you one."

Clint looked up at Hartman with a frown on his face. His face was marked with some cuts and bruises, but on the whole he hadn't been seriously injured.

"All right, damn it, what do you want me to read?"

"This," Hartman said, extending the newspaper to him. "that is, unless you want me to read it to you."

"I can read," Clint snapped, grabbing the paper. "What page?"

"Front headline, pal. Front headline is really going to interest you."

Denson knew what Hartman meant, because he'd already seen the headline.

Both men watched the Gunsmith while he read, and saw the change that came over his face.

"Damn," Clint whispered, "damn, damn... *damn!*" The last was a shout, and he crumpled the newspaper in his hands and squeezed it tight.

"They cut him loose?" he asked, the disbelief plain in his tone. "They let Bill's murderer go free?"

"They acquitted him," Hartman said, "in a court of law." He reached down and took the crumpled newspaper from Clint Adam's hand, and asked him, "Do you still want that drink now?"

TWO

It was easier for Clint Adams to come back physically than it was for him to do it mentally. He'd lost some weight, and the constant drinking had given his hands the shakes, but some decent meals and cutting off the whiskey altogether fixed that up in a couple of weeks.

"You look better," Rick Hartman told him in mid-September.

"I feel better," Clint replied. "I could even have a beer if I wanted one."

"Do you?" Hartman asked, looking towards the bartender.

"No."

Hartman nodded and examined Clint. He had put some of the weight back on. He was clean-shaven and had recently bathed. His eyes were clear and his hands were steady.

"You leaving?"

"Yes."

"Have they found McCall yet?"

"Not yet."

"Where will you go?"

"To Deadwood."

"Good luck," Hartman said, putting his hand out.

"Thanks," Clint said, taking the hand. Then he added, "Thanks for everything, Rick."

"Don't mention it. Just watch your step...and stop around again, when you can."

Hartman watched as the Gunsmith left his place; he wondered if he'd ever see or hear from the man again.

Clint wondered about his mental well-being as he rode out of Labyrinth, Texas. Physically, he felt almost fully recovered. A few more pounds and he'd be back to normal.

But mentally—even he wasn't sure, and that was a new feeling for Clint Adams. He was not used to being unsure of himself, but then he hadn't been himself for some time.

He understood how he could feel grief and an overwhelming sense of loss at hearing about the death of Wild Bill, but what he couldn't understand was the rest of it. The drinking, the constant drinking, and allowing himself to get to the point where he couldn't even draw his gun without dropping it.

What the hell had driven him to that?

He was sure that the cause was something inside of himself, something he could not yet see or explain. He didn't have time, however, to stop and search himself for the answer. First he had to find Bill's killer and make sure he did not go free, and to do that he had to start in Deadwood.

He just hoped that when the time came for him to take care of Jack McCall, the unnamed something that was still eating away at his insides did not get in the way.

He grinned ironically to himself as he directed his team onto the main road. For years he had been trying to overcome his reputation as the Gunsmith, and now he hoped that he still had the stuff that had earned him that name in the first place.

THREE

Deadwood, Dakota Territory

Deadwood—or Deadwood Gulch—was actually a dead-end canyon, bordered by a mountain stream and a steep rock wall. It housed a mining town that was split into three camps: Elizabeth City, Crook City and Deadwood City. Deadwood City was the largest and most notorious of the three.

It was here that Bill Hickok had been killed.

The town consisted basically of one main street, which was lined with some stores, hotels and other places of business, but mostly saloons. All of these had literally been thrown together from whatever materials were at hand and needed constant repairs and reinforcements to keep them standing.

The Gunsmith directed his wagon down the congested street, which was lined with people, horses, mules and wagons, and was so choked with traffic that there was a permanent dust cloud filling the air.

Just in riding from the beginning of town to the livery stable, Clint received a half a dozen offers to buy his big black horse, Duke, all of which he naturally turned down. As a result, however, he was determined to make certain Duke was watched at all times. Not that he was concerned that the horse would be stolen; he just didn't want Duke stomping to death anyone who might have a notion to try.

At the livery Clint hopped down from his rig and gave the liveryman instructions.

"I don't want anybody going near my horse," he told the grizzled old-timer who was in charge.

"Lots of people in and out of here, mister—"

"Nobody goes near that horse, Pop," Clint said coldly, and the old man backed off.

"What about me?"

"You can unsaddle him, rub him down and feed him, but don't try to ride him, and don't let anyone near him. Understand?"

"Sure, mister, sure. You can count on me."

Clint took his rifle and saddlebags, then asked the old man, "Where's the nearest hotel?"

"Just make a left here and walk about a block. That's the closest, and they're pretty much all the same in Deadwood."

"Yeah," Clint said. "Thanks."

Atta boy, Clint, he told himself, walking down the street. *Prove you've still got it by scaring the pants off an old man.*

When he reached the hotel he asked the desk clerk, "Got a room?"

"I might," the kid answered. He was about twenty-four or so, and he had a cocky attitude that didn't suit Clint in his present mood.

He put down his rifle and saddlebags, leaned on

the counter and said, "Well, I just might want one."

"And I might let you have one," the kid replied, "for the right price."

Clint reached out and grabbed the front of the kid's shirt and pulled him halfway across the desk. "For the right price, sonny, I won't drag you the rest of the way across the desk and throw you through the window. What do you say to that?"

"Okay, mister, okay," the kid said. "You don't have to get rough. You want a room, you got a room."

"Fine," Clint said. He released his hold on the kid's shirt and the kid almost fell when his feet hit the floor.

"Something overlooking the street," Clint told him.

"Sure, mister. Would you mind signing in?"

"Give me the book."

The kid passed him the register and Clint signed his name.

"What room?" he asked, reversing the book.

"Number four, at the top of the stairs. Looks out over the street, just like you want."

"Thanks," Clint said, snatching the key from the kid's hand.

"Sure, Mr.—" the kid began, then he stopped and took a look at the register. With widened eyes, he looked back at Clint and his mouth fell open.

"What's your problem?" Clint asked.

"Nothing, Mr. A-Adams, nothing at all. Uh, ain't you the one they call, uh, the G-Gunsmith, though?"

"You call me by whatever name I signed in the register," Clint said. "That's all you need to know."

"Sure, mister—uh, sure."

As Clint went up the stairs, the young clerk's head swiveled back and forth as he looked for some—anyone—that he could tell, but there was no one around.

Jeez, the kid thought, *first Hickok, and now the Gunsmith*. As if this place didn't have enough excitement.

Upstairs, Clint dropped his saddlebags on a chair, leaned his rifle against the wall, and then unstrapped his gun and hung it on the bedpost. He walked to the window and looked out at the dusty main street of Deadwood.

What a place to die, Bill, he thought. *I know you didn't pick it, but there must have been some way to avoid it.*

He opened one side of his saddlebags and took out two crumpled newspapers. One had the account of Hickok's death, and the other had the story of his killer's acquittal. Clint read them both over once again for the hundredth time.

Bill had been playing poker in a saloon known only as No. 10. Jack McCall had come up behind him and fired once, striking him in the head. Also wounded at the time was a man named Captain William Massey, yet only one shot had reportedly been fired. The bartender stated that McCall had also tried to fire at him, but the gun had misfired.

The other paper simply stated that McCall had been found innocent of all charges and had been set free. Soon after, it said, he had left Deadwood.

Clint, a lawman for many years, couldn't understand how McCall could have been acquitted if there had been witnesses to the killing.

Surely the bartender and Massey could have testified and whoever else had been in the game, as well.

He didn't believe that justice could be that blind, so there was only one answer. The court that had set McCall free had been rigged. Clint felt it was up to him to find McCall and make sure he got a genuine trial in a real court of law. Of course, it would be up to McCall himself whether he'd come back alive . . . or dead. Clint would give the man the right to choose how he wanted to die, which was more than McCall had given Bill Hickok.

He stuffed the paper back in the saddlebags and decided that it was time to have a beer. He intended to stay away from whiskey for a little longer, but a beer to wash away the trail dust wouldn't hurt.

Especially if he had it at the saloon called No. 10.

FOUR

The Gunsmith figured his first step would be to
talk to the witnesses: the bartender at the No. 10 and
Captain Massey, for a start. From them he could get
the names of the others. It might also be a good idea
to talk to the local law.

That was when he got a surprise.

"Hey, kid," he said to the desk clerk.

"Yes, sir?"

"Who's the sheriff in this town?"

"Ain't no sheriff, Mr. Adams."

"Then who's the law? Who keeps the peace?"

The kid started to laugh, then caught himself. "There
ain't much peace around here, neither, Mr. Adams,
but while he was alive, Wild Bill sort of appointed
himself as marshal."

"He did, huh?" The last time Clint had seen Hickok

21

for any length of time had been in Abilene,* and it
was then he'd realized that Bill had been having trouble
with his eyes. If he had appointed himself, he
must have had a deputy to back his play.

"Did he have an unofficial deputy?"

"Sure—I guess Charlie Utter would have fit that
bill."

"Who?"

"Colorado Charlie Utter. He came into town with
Bill when Bill first got here."

"Okay, kid. Thanks."

"Sure, Mr. Adams, anytime."

The kid knew who he was, so it wouldn't be long
before it would be all over town—the town where
Bill Hickok was killed. Somebody was bound to try
him, he knew. He would rather get all the information
he needed and get out of Deadwood before that happened.

He made his way through the crowded streets to
No. 10, which was doing a booming business, no
doubt as a result of the publicity. He shouldered his
way to the bar and ordered a beer.

"Just get in?" the bartender asked.

"It shows, huh?" Clint asked.

"After a while it gets so you can tell," the man
answered.

"Is this where it happened?" Clint asked.

"Yeah," the bartender said, shaking his head.
"That's what most people have been asking. This is
where it happened, all right, but I'd just as soon not
talk about it anymore."

"Why not?"

*The Gunsmith #4, Guns of Abilene

The bartender leaned on the bar and said, "Bill was all right, as far as I'm concerned. When they let Jack McCall loose, it was like throwing mud on Bill's name, you know?"

"You saw the whole thing?"

"I saw it, all right. McCall just came up behind Bill and shot him dead. The bullet went right through his head and hit Captain Massey in the arm. Massey was so shocked he thought Bill shot him, but he should have knowed better than that."

"Why?"

"Them two have been good friends for a long time. The other players in the game were his friends too."

"Who were they?"

"Charlie Rich and Carl Mann."

Clint knew Rich. He was a gunman and a gambler, and supposedly was good at both.

"Who's Mann?"

The bartender frowned, just now starting to wonder why the stranger was asking so many questions, but he answered anyway.

"Mr. Mann owns No. 10."

"I see," Clint said, nodding. "What's your name?"

"Harry Young. And you're—?"

"Adams. Clint Adams."

The bartender reacted, raising his eyebrows and then almost shouted, "Of course, you're—"

"Clint Adams," Clint said, interrupting him before he could go any further.

"Uh, yeah, right," Harry Young said. "It's nice to meet you. Bill used to talk about you."

"Uh-huh. Where can I find Mr. Mann?"

"In his office, in the back."

"Should I be announced?"

"Naw, just go and knock on the door—but not too hard, you might bring the whole place down on our heads."

"I'll remember," Clint said. He picked up his beer, said, "Thanks, Harry," and started for the back of the room.

He knocked gently at the door in the back and entered when a voice from behind invited him to.

"Can I help you?"

"Are you Carl Mann?" Clint asked the man seated behind the desk. He was about thirty-five, with fair hair and a bushy mustache.

"That's me, friend. What can I do for you? Something wrong with the beer?"

"The beer's fine," Clint said, approaching the desk. "I'd like to talk to you about Bill Hickok."

"Hickok's dead," Mann said flatly, dropping his pleasant manner.

"I know that," Clint said. "I want to find the man who did it."

"Everybody knows Jack McCall did it."

"Then why was he acquitted?"

Mann frowned at Clint and said, "Who are you, friend?"

"Clint Adams."

Recognition washed over Mann's features, and he sat forward in his chair.

"The Gunsmith," he said. Clint winced but let it pass.

"Why was McCall acquitted?" Clint asked again.

"Who knows?" Mann said, sitting uneasily. He had heard Hickok talk of the Gunsmith many times. Bill had allowed as he had never seen a man draw and fire as quickly and as accurately as Clint Adams. Mann knew that Adams's rep was as a lawman *and* gunman. Bill had said that Adams was no killer, but his presence still made Mann very nervous.

"Take a guess," Clint said.

Mann sat back now, although he was unable to relax, and said, "A payoff, then—at least, that's what Colonel May thought."

"Who's May?"

"He was the prosecutor. Was he hot when the jury came in with the verdict! He said he'd dog McCall's trail until he could try him in a real court of law, and not a miner's court."

It sounded to Clint like he and this Colonel May were on the same side. "Where can I find May?"

"He left town soon after McCall did."

That figured. "How about Charlie Rich and Charlie Utter?"

"Rich is in town, I think. Probably Colorado Charlie, too. He pretty much crawled into a bottle after the trial. He and Bill were good friends."

That sounded familiar. "What hotel is Rich at?"

"Down the block. Make a right when you walk out, and go to the end. It hasn't got a name."

"Or a number?"

"Nothing."

"And Captain Massey?"

"Same hotel."

"Okay," Clint said, setting the empty beer mug on Mann's table. "You were there when it happened?"

"I was. We were playing poker."

"And it was McCall?"

"No doubt."

"What about Massey? How bad was he hurt?"

"Not bad. The bullet caught him in the forearm."

"Why'd he accuse Bill?"

"He didn't actually accuse him," Mann said. "It

all happened so fast, and Massey just kind of panicked."

"I see," Clint said, standing up. "All right, Mr.
Mann, thanks for the information."

As Clint headed for the door Mann called out to
him. "Are you going to look for McCall?"

"I am."

"What will you do with him when you catch him?"
Mann asked. He said *when* because from Adams's
attitude and from everything Bill had said about him,
Mann was sure that he would.

Clint opened the door and before leaving answered,
"That'll be up to him."

FIVE

Clint left the saloon and walked down to the hotel where Massey and Rich were supposedly staying.

"Captain Massey's room," he said to the clerk. This one was ancient and hadn't been cocky for at least forty years.

"Second floor, room six."

"And Charlie Rich?"

The old man's eyes changed and he said, "That's a little different, friend. Rich wouldn't like it if—"

"Pop, I'm here and he's not, and I won't like it if you don't give me his room number."

The old man saw what was in Clint Adams's eyes, and he said, "Third floor, room twelve."

"Thanks," Clint said. Ascending the stairs he scolded himself. *Old men and children*, he thought. *What's next, kicking dogs?*

He went to the second floor first, to see Massey.

27

When he found room 6 he knocked and heard a groan from inside.

"Massey!" he called out.

"Who's it?" a voice called out.

"I'm coming in," Clint said. He tried the door, found it unlocked and entered.

Massey, a tall, thin, gray-haired man, was lying on his bed with a bottle of whiskey in his right hand. His left hand was lying next to him, unmoving. Clint was able to make put a small section of bandage sticking out beyond the cuff.

"I don't like to stand in hotel hallways, shouting out my name," he told the tall man. "It's not healthy."

"Now that you're in," Massey said, "who are you?"

"A friend of Bill Hickok's."

"The wake is over, friend," Massey said

"I'd like to ask you a few questions."

"Go ahead and ask."

"Did you see McCall shoot Bill?"

"If I had, I wouldn't't've run from that saloon shouting that Bill had shot me," Massey answered, shaking his head. "What a dumb move. No, I couldn't see McCall. The little weasel was standing behind Bill."

"Did you hear him say anything?"

"Bill?"

"McCall."

"I didn't think so at the time, but later I realized that he had shouted something just before I heard the shot. Something like 'Take that.'"

"Did you know McCall?"

"Only to nod to, or play cards with," Massey said. He took a pull from the bottle, then said, "Lousy card player. Dropped his poke to Bill the night before. Bill gave him money for breakfast, but the ungrateful weasel thought that Bill was just rubbing it in."

"Was McCall alone?"

"Yes."

"I don't mean in the saloon," Clint said. "I mean, was killing Bill his idea, or was he put up to it?"

"Put up to it?" Massey asked. "There's a thought, but I really couldn't tell you."

"Who could?"

"I don't know."

"Charlie Rich?"

"Did you talk to Charlie?"

"Not yet. I will when I leave here."

"Charlie's been irritable lately," Massey said.

Clint stood up and said, "So have I, Captain. Thanks for the conversation."

"Sure."

As Clint crossed the room to leave Massey asked, "What did you say your name was?"

"I didn't," Clint said, "but it's Adams."

He left the room, having no interest at all in what Massey's reaction was to his name.

He walked up to the third floor and knocked on the door to room 12.

"Yeah?"

"Charlie Rich?"

"Who wants to know?"

"I'd rather come in and tell you."

A pause, and then, "Come ahead then, but keep your hands where I can see them."

Clint opened the door, then stepped in with his hands held out in front of him.

Rich was standing next to the bed, but out of line with the window. *A careful man,* Clint thought. *Like Bill . . . was.*

"Who are you?" Rich asked. He was a dark man. Dark skin, dark eyes, dark, unruly hair.

"Clint Adams."

Rich's eyebrows went up, and his gun—which had been trained on the Gunsmith's belly—went down.

"Why the hell didn't you say so?" Rich asked. "Put your hands down and find someplace to sit."

"Thanks."

"Drink?" Rich asked, picking up a half-empty bottle from the floor by the bed.

"No, thanks."

Rich shrugged, holstered his gun, and took a drink from the bottle. "I guess there's no point in asking you why you're here."

"No," Clint said. "I came to find out the truth about Bill's death."

"What's to find out? Everybody knows what happened."

"I know McCall shot him, and I know he was acquitted."

"A little gold dust in the jury room fixed that up real nice," Rich said.

"Who paid it?"

"You got me."

"So then McCall wasn't on his own?"

"Somebody paid his way out," Rich said, "but I don't know if that means he was put up to it—if that's what you mean."

"That's what I mean."

Rich shrugged and took another drink.

"What's the story with Charlie Utter?"

"He took it hard," Rich said, "started drinking . . . heavily."

"I'd like to talk to him."

"Think you can get through to him?"

Clint smiled grimly and said, "I know I can. Where would he be?"

"He could be anywhere."

"That helps."

"Sorry, Adams, but that's all I've got."

"Okay," Clint said. "Tell me why Bill wasn't sitting with his back to the wall."

"Somebody was sitting there already. Bill asked for the seat a couple of times, but they wouldn't budge."

"Who was sitting there?" Clint asked.

"Massey," Rich said. "Captain Massey."

"Was Bill's back facing the entrance?"

"No, his back was to the bar. McCall came in through the front doors, walked around the table once, and when he got behind Bill again he pulls out his big forty-five, shouts 'Take that,' and fires into Bill's head."

"How'd Massey get hurt if only one shot was fired?"

"The bullet passed through Bill's head and hit Massey in the left forearm," Rich said. "He was so shocked, he thought Bill shot him."

"So I heard."

Rich took another drink and said, "A damned shame, but I guess men like Bill, you and me, we'll all go like that one of these days."

"Not me," Clint said coldly, standing up.

"You ain't gonna die in bed, friend," Rich said. "Not with your reputation."

"That may be," Clint said, "but I'm not going to die from a bullet in the back, either. A bullet fired by a coward!"

Clint felt the rage building up inside of him, and his hands were beginning to shake.

"I guess that's it," Clint said, making for the door.

"You need anything else, you let me know," Rich said. "We're the same kind, you, me and Bill. The same kind."

"Thanks."

Out in the hall, Clint stood with his back to the wall and waited for the rage to fade. Once it did, and his hands had stopped shaking, he walked down the hall, wondering who the rage had been directed at: McCall for killing Bill, at Bill for allowing himself to be killed—or was it directed at himself?

Maybe it went back to that thing that was still inside of him, but he still didn't have time to think about it.

He had to talk to Massey again, and he had to try and find Colorado Charlie Utter.

The man sounded like someone he could get along with.

SIX

Massey had either left his room in search of another bottle, or he knew that Clint was going to find out that he had refused to give Wild Bill his seat. Either way, Clint would now have to search for both Colorado Charlie and Captain Massey. He didn't think Massey was the type to have set Hickok up, but he did want to know why Massey had refused to give him the seat.

Colorado Charlie did not prove hard to find. Clint started at one end of Deadwood and worked his way through the saloons until he found him sitting underneath a table with a partly full bottle of rotgut.

Utter had been pointed out to Clint by the bartender, and Clint approached him.

Crouching down he asked, "Are you Charlie Utter?"

Utter, with one eye closed, peered out from under

the table at Clint and said, "Colorado Charlie, friend, that's me. You got a fresh bottle?"

"No," Clint said. He took the bottle from Utter's hand and upended it, pouring the whiskey out onto the floor.

"What the hell did you do that for?" Utter demanded.

"We have a mutual friend, Charlie," Clint told him, "and he needs us. Come on."

He put his hand out to help the man from under the table, but apparently Utter didn't want to come out.

"What friend?" he demanded.

"Wild Bill Hickok."

Utter frowned drunkenly, and for a moment Clint thought that he hadn't understood.

Then the man said, "Bill's dead."

"I know," Clint said, "and his killer's gone free. I want to find McCall, Charlie, and I need your help."

"McCall," Utter said, his frown deepening.

"Come on, Charlie," Clint said, grabbing the man's hand, "we have to talk."

"Where are we going?"

"To a hotel."

"I don't have a room."

"I do," Clint assured him. He half-dragged Utter from under the table, and as he turned to walk him out of the saloon, his path was barred by a big man.

"Hey, Charlie," the man said, "need another bottle?"

Utter opened his mouth to answer, but Clint beat him to it.

"No, he doesn't."

The man, who was taller than Clint, but running to fat, said, "Hey, friend, I asked Colorado Charlie."

"And I answered," Clint said. "Now please move out of the way."

Clint started to move past the man, but the big man sidestepped into his path.

"Not until my friend Charlie answers me."

"Look, friend—" Clint said, but next to him Charlie moved too fast for either him or the big man to react. Utter brought his knee up hard between the big man's legs and for a moment the big man did not react. Then his eyes went wide, his mouth opened, and as he grabbed his testicles he began to fall forward. Clint and Utter moved out of the way and the man went to his knees on the hardwood floor. Utter then swung his elbow back so that it struck the back of the man's head, driving him face first into the floor.

Utter looked at Clint proudly and said, "Let's go."

"Anything you say," Clint replied, and they left the saloon and headed for Clint's hotel.

SEVEN

When they got to Clint's room Utter asked, "Do you have a drink?"

"No," Clint said. "I've had enough for a while, and so have you. I need you sober."

"Sober," Utter repeated.

"Yes, sober," Clint said. He pointed to the pitcher and basin and said, "Wash your face."

"Wash?"

"Yes, Charlie, wash, damn it! Come on, we have to talk and I want your replies to make some sense."

Utter, who was beyond any serious resistance, went over to the basin, filled it with water from the pitcher, and then dipped his hands in it. He leaned over it and barely touched his hands to his face. Clint came up behind him and pushed his face into the pitcher of water, submerging his nose and mouth. Utter was a pretty big man, but his drinking binge had robbed him of much of his strength, a condition Clint knew very well. He held Utter's face under water for a few moments, then took his hand away.

Utter came up choking and gasping for air, and considerably more sober than he had been moments before.

"Jesus," he shouted, "what the hell—"

He turned to face Clint and swung his right fist at him. Clint sidestepped and then poleaxed Utter in the middle of the chest with the palm of his right hand.

The blow pushed Utter back a few steps until he hit the table with the basin of water, upsetting it. Utter kept his feet—just barely—and stood glaring at Clint.

"You were a friend of Bill's?" he asked.

"Yup."

"What's your name?"

"Clint Adams?"

"Shit," Utter said. He wiped his sleeve across his face to dry it, then sniffed and said, "Shit," again.

"You know me?" Clint asked.

"I heard tell of you, yeah," Utter admitted. "Bill talked about you sometimes."

"Were you a friend of Bill's?"

"Shit, yeah," he said. "Me'n Bill shot together more times than I kin count. I beat him more times than not, too."

"You outshot Bill?" Clint asked, frowning.

"I kin hit a dime at a hundred feet nine times out of ten," Utter bragged. "Couldn't match Bill for speed, though," he admitted. "Nobody can." He paused a moment, then added, "'Ceptin' maybe you, to hear Bill tell it."

"Bill was faster than God," Clint said.

"Damn," Utter said, "but that's what he used to say about you." Utter wiped the rest of his face dry, stood up straight and said, "I guess you are who you say you are. Mind if I set?"

"No, go ahead."

Utter sat in the only chair in the room, and Clint took off his hat and sat on the bed.

"I heard about Bill getting killed about six weeks ago," Clint said, "maybe more. I did just what you did."

"Took to drinkin'?"

Clint nodded. "But that don't matter now," Clint said, since he still didn't have time to study on it. "What matters is that Jack McCall got away with killing Bill, and we can't let that happen."

"We got to set it right," Utter said, and Clint nodded. "How are we gonna do that?"

"You're going to tell me which way Jack McCall went when he left here, and then I'm going to take off after him."

"All you want me to do is tell you which way he went?"

"That's right," Clint said. "I figure before you started in on the bottle, you followed him a ways. Why you didn't go after him is your business, but I want to know which way he went."

Utter wiped a stray drop of water from his nose and then said, "He went west . . . and that Colonel May went right after him."

"West? Towards Wyoming?"

"Less'n he took to going north after a ways, and headed for Montana," Utter said.

"What do you figure?" Clint asked.

"I figure Wyoming," Utter said, "and then maybe on through to Nevada. That's where McCall claimed Bill shot and killed his brother. Course, nobody believed him."

"Except the jury," Clint pointed out.

Utter made a derisive noise and said, "The jury believed in gold dust and nothin' else."

"Wyoming it is, then," Clint said.

"When you plan on leaving?"

"In the morning," Clint said. "Quicker I get out of Deadwood, the better."

"Mind if I ride along?"

"You got a horse?"

"Yup."

"Why do you want to come?"

Rubbing his jaw, Utter said, "To tell you the plumb truth, Adams, I'm ashamed of the way I been acting. Figure I owe it to Ole Jim to make sure his killer don't get off scot-free, like that."

"Ole Jim" was Bill's nickname from his full name of James Butler Hickok. Clint didn't rightly know how he came to be called "Wild Bill," but that's what most people called him.

"You be able to stay off the whiskey?"

"I will," Utter said, without hesitating.

"I guess you can come along, then," Clint said, standing up. "Got a place to spend the night?"

"I was aimin' to spend it under that table, but that spot's liable to be gone by now."

"You snore?"

"Only when I'm dead drunk."

"You can sleep on the floor," Clint said. "We'll start out at first light."

"Fine by me, Adams."

"Call me Clint."

"You kin call me Charlie, I reckon. Most folks do."

"Okay, Charlie," Clint said, unstrapping his gun and hanging it on the bedpost. "Let's get some sleep."

A few minutes later, when the lamp had been turned down, Charlie said, "Clint?"

"Yeah?"

"Reckon I oughta thank you for getting me out from under that table."

"You would have gotten out yourself sooner or later," Clint said.

"Yeah," Utter said, "but later might have been too late. Much obliged."

"Go to sleep, Charlie," Clint said. "Just go to sleep."

EIGHT

Laramie City, Wyoming Territory

The man seated in the back of the Laramie Saloon appeared to be somewhere around forty years old. He was a thin, scruffy-looking individual who was actually only twenty-five or so, but a life of being broke and living hand to mouth had made him old before his time.

This was Jack McCall.

McCall was holding court now, and he was enjoying the notoriety that was his as a result of having killed Bill Hickok.

He made no secret of the fact that he had shot Hickok in the back of the head, because he was confident that he could not be tried for the same crime twice.

So, very drunkenly and very loudly, he was telling all who cared to listen how he had killed Wild Bill Hickok and had gotten away with it.

"They couldn't put old Jack McCall away, because I had the guts to do what nobody else would," he was saying as the batwing doors opened and a man wearing a badge walked in.

Sheriff Ben Lomax had heard about McCall and his brag, and having a man in his town who was proud of having backshot a man, especially a man like Wild Bill Hickok, rubbed against the lawman's grain.

He approached McCall now and said, "Excuse me."

"Howdy, Sheriff," McCall greeted. "And what can I do for you?"

"Are you the man who claims to have killed Bill Hickok?"

"Claims?" McCall said indignantly. "Are you saying that I'm not a man of my word, Sheriff?"

"I'm not saying anything," Lomax said. "I'm just asking you if you're the man says he killed Bill Hickok."

"I certainly am," McCall said. "I killed the greatest gunman in the world, and I got away with it, and there ain't nothin' that nobody can do about it."

"Do you have a gun, McCall?" the sheriff asked.

"A gun?" McCall asked. "Why would I need a gun?"

"I don't know," the sheriff said. "Do you?"

"No, sir, I don't," McCall said. He slid his chair back and spread open his dirty coat.

"All right, McCall," the lawman said, picking the man's hat up from the table and throwing it into his lap. "Let's go."

"Go? Go where?" McCall asked.

"You're under arrest."

"What for?"

"For the murder of Wild Bill Hickok."

McCall laughed and said, "I already been tried for

that one, Sheriff. You can't arrest me."

Lomas drew his gun and pointed it at McCall's nose.

"You still telling me what I can't do?"

"H-hey, wait—" McCall stammered, but the lawman gave him no time to go on.

"I been a lawman for a lot of years, McCall, and I can't believe that a proper court of law could have made such a mistake as to have set you free. While you're warming one of my cells, we'll be looking into just what kind of a trial you really had in Deadwood. Up on your feet."

"Hey—"

Lomax cocked his gun and said, "I'm not gonna tell you again, man. Get up!"

McCall, shaken but stubborn, got up and said, "You'll see, Sheriff. I been tried fair and proper, and set free. You'll see."

"Walk," the sheriff said, prodding McCall with his gun, and he marched the scruffy little killer over to his jail and deposited him in a cell.

The local judge in Laramie City, Wyoming set down a ruling that Jack McCall had been tried in a miner's court, which was not a duly recognized court of law, according to constituted law. He therefore remanded McCall to custody and ordered that he be removed to Yankton, the capital of the Dakota Territory, for a lawful and proper trial on the charge of murder.

When Clint Adams and Colorado Charlie Utter were crossing the border between South Dakota and Wyoming, Jack McCall was on a train to Yankton, complaining every step of the way.

NINE

Clint Adams and Colorado Charlie Utter rode into Laramie City, Wyoming a full day after Jack McCall had left, accompanied by a federal deputy marshal.

Before leaving Deadwood, Clint had been unable to locate Captain Massey and had also discovered that Charlie Rich left town. During the ride from Deadwood to Laramie City, Clint also found out something else from Colorado Charlie.

Captain Massey had not been the man sitting with his back to the wall. It had been Charlie Rich.

"Who told you it was Massey?" Charlie asked as they rode along.

"Rich."

Charlie Utter shook his head and said, "No, it was Rich. He asked Bill if he was that superstitious and said he wouldn't give up his seat."

"Why?"

47

"Who knows? Maybe Rich was the one who was superstitious."

"Could Rich have been setting Bill up?"

"I don't see how or why," Charlie answered.

"If somebody did put McCall up to killing Bill, who would it have been?"

"Probably Johnny Varnes and Tim Brady."

"Who are they?"

"Just a couple of town toughs who didn't like the idea of Bill appointing himself unofficial marshal."

"Are they gunmen?"

"No, just hardcases."

"They wouldn't face Bill on their own, so they sent McCall to backshoot him."

"That's the way I figure it."

"Where are they?"

Charlie Utter shrugged and said, "I looked for them right after McCall was arrested, but I think they high-tailed it out of town."

Clint filed their names away in the back of his mind for future reference. McCall pulled the trigger, so he was at the head of the list.

When they arrived in Laramie City, they put the horses up at the livery, and Clint started thinking about boarding his rig and team if they had to leave town for any reason. He hadn't wanted to leave the rig in Deadwood, but Laramie City seemed to be a pretty peaceful town, and he could always come back for the rig later.

"Let's get to the hotel," Clint said as they left the livery.

"How about the saloon?" Charlie Utter asked.

"After the hotel," Clint said, "and then only for a beer."

"Sure," Charlie said. "No whiskey."

"Not until we're finished."

"Right."

They stopped at the nearest hotel, and Clint arranged for a room for each of them. Charlie had very little money, so while he rode with the Gunsmith, Clint was picking up the expenses. It was worth it, simply to have Utter along to identify McCall when they found him.

As he handed Charlie his key, Utter asked, "What now?"

"You can go to the saloon, Charlie," Clint said.

"Where are you going?"

"I'm going to check in with the local law. I'll meet you over there in a little while."

"Okay," Utter said, starting for the door. He had no gear to put in his room, traveling with only the clothes he was wearing, his six-guns and his rifle, which he kept with him. He was a much better rifle shot than he was a pistol shot, and he kept his Henry with him everyplace he went.

"Charlie," Clint called out, stopping the man before he could get out the door.

"Yeah?"

"One beer."

"Oh, sure, Clint," he agreed. "One beer."

Clint went up to his room to leave his rifle and saddlebags, but before leaving he removed his little .22 Colt New Line from his saddlebag and tucked into his belt, inside his shirt. Comfortably armed, he left the hotel and went in search of the local jailhouse.

He got directions from the desk clerk and found the sheriff's office fairly easily. There was a sign outside that told him the sheriff's name was Ben Lomax. He entered the office without knocking.

"Sheriff Lomax?"

"That's right," a man behind the desk said. "What can I do for you?"

"I just got into town, Sheriff," Clint said, approaching the desk. "My name is Clint Adams."

"Adams, huh?" Lomax said, rubbing his jaw. "I've heard of you. What are you doing in Laramie City, Adams?"

"Tracking a man," Clint answered. "I've tracked him from Deadwood, and the trail leads here. I'd like to know if you've seen him, and whether he's moved on or is still here."

"What's your interest in this man?" Lomax asked.

"He killed a friend of mine."

"You totin' a badge? Seems to me I heard you gave up carrying a badge."

"I have, and I'm not wearing one now," Clint answered. "This is personal."

"What do you aim on doing if you catch up to this man?"

"I figure that'll be up to him, Sheriff."

"I don't want any killing in my town, Adams. If that's what you came here for, you can just mount up and ride out again."

"The man's name is Jack McCall, Sheriff," Clint went on, undaunted. "Maybe you've heard of him."

"Sure, I've heard of him, and if that's the case, you might as well mount up and ride out anyway."

"Why? Was he here?"

"He was, and now he's gone."

"Gone where?" Clint demanded.

Lomax studied Clint for a few moments, then said, "So you and Hickok were friends, huh?"

"Good friends, Sheriff, and I don't like the idea of the man who backshot him getting off scot-free."

"Well, to tell you the truth, Adams, that idea didn't

appeal much to me, either." Lomax leaned back in his chair and continued. "Yeah, he was here for a while. He was holding court in the saloon, bragging about how he gunned down Bill Hickok and got away with it."

Clint felt the anger welling up inside of him and found himself wondering why it was just anger and not that rage again.

"What happened?"

"I arrested him."

"You arrested him?" Clint asked. "For what?"

"For murder," Lomax said. "I didn't like the idea of him coming to my town and bragging that he put one over on the law. We took him into court, and Judge Waters decided that the miner's court that found him innocent in Deadwood was not a true and legal court of law."

Clint, who had upheld the law for eighteen years or so, felt a brief surge of satisfaction at hearing that.

"What happened to him?"

"He was sent to Yankton for a new and legal trial," Lomax said. "He left yesterday."

"Yesterday!" Clint said, bitterly.

"That's right, Adams," Lomax said, leaning forward. "You missed him by one day, and judging by the look in your eye when you talk about him, maybe it's just as well. You might have ended up being the one I arrested for murder."

TEN

Clint went to the saloon and explained the situation to Colorado Charlie, who was nursing a beer. After that, he ordered beer and he and Charlie sat in silence, with their own thoughts.

McCall had been arrested once before and then set free. Who was to say that it couldn't happen again? And then there were the two toughs, Varnes and Brady, who had probably put McCall up to the killing. From what he'd heard about Jack McCall, he was convinced that the man was a coward and would have needed someone behind him, pushing him to do his dirty deed.

"We're going to Yankton," he told Utter.

"What for?"

"To watch McCall's new trial," he answered, "and to see if Varnes and Brady show up too."

"Why would they?"

"If they're afraid that McCall will mention their names, they might try something during the trial . . . and I also want to be there just in case history repeats itself."

"What do you mean?"

"What if McCall is acquitted again?" he asked Charlie.

"They wouldn't do that—"

"It happened once, it can happen again," Clint said. "And if it does, I want to be right there"—he put his hand out in front of him—"where I can just put my hand out and reach him.

"Drink up. We'll leave for Yankton in the morning." As Charlie picked the beer up and moved it towards his mouth, Clint said, "And nurse it. It'll be the last one you get for a while."

Clint picked up his own beer and took a medium-sized sip, to wash the dust from his throat. He felt oddly calm at that moment. He knew where McCall was, and knew that he would be there for a while, until he himself arrived in Yankton. He would sit and watch as the trial progressed, knowing that, just in case McCall once again succeeded in putting one over on the law, he'd be there to make sure that justice was done, one way or another.

ELEVEN

Yankton, Dakota Territory

At the same time, in a saloon in Yankton, two men were also discussing the upcoming new trial of Jack McCall for the charge of the murder of Wild Bill Hickok.

"I thought a man couldn't be tried for the same crime twice," Tim Brady complained.

"Well, they're doing it," Johnny Varnes said. "What we got to worry about now is McCall giving them our names."

"We didn't pull no trigger," Brady pointed out.

"No, but we—uh—*encouraged* McCall to go and do it. We could be what they call guilty of a conspiracy, or something like that."

"Shit," Brady said, "for all the trouble we're having now, we should have shot Hickok ourselves."

"Yeah, only we never would have gotten behind him like that," Varnes pointed out. "Who would have believed a nobody like McCall would be planning to kill Hickok? That's the only reason McCall got away with it."

"Only he ain't got away with it," Brady said. "Not yet."

They were seated together at the corner table with a bottle of whiskey, and nobody in Yankton had any idea who they were or that they had ever been in Deadwood, and Johnny Varnes wanted to keep it that way.

"We got to keep low, Tim," Varnes told his partner. "If things look bad for McCall and we think he's gonna give out our names, we're gonna have to take care of him."

"Kill him, you mean?"

"Yeah, kill him," Varnes said. "And this time we will do it ourselves. If we do it right, the law will just think that some friend of Hickok wanted revenge."

Brady laughed at that and said, "Imagine anybody thinking we was friends of Hickok's!"

"It's a lucky thing we was in Wyoming when McCall was arrested again," Varnes said, "or we wouldn't know what the hell was going on until it was too late. At least now we'll be here when his trial starts, and be able to keep an eye open."

"And if he looks like he's gonna say the wrong thing," Brady said, making like he had a gun in his hand, "bang!"

TWELVE

When Clint Adams and Colorado Charlie rode into Yankton, they put up their horses in the livery—Clint had indeed left his rig and team in Laramie—and then they went to a small hotel where they took two rooms.

"I'm going to leave my gear in my room, and then go over and check in with the law," he told Charlie.

"You gonna find out where they're holding McCall?"

Clint nodded and added, "And when his trial is set for."

"I'll meet you at the saloon across the street," Charlie said.

Clint hesitated a moment, then said, "One beer, Charlie, and that's it."

"Whatever you say, Clint."

Yankton had a sheriff and a marshal, so Clint went to see Federal Marshal Jeff Hanks.

"I've heard of you, Adams," Hanks said, "Used to be a damned good lawman, until you packed it in."

"Everybody's got to pack it in sometime, Marshal."

"Depends on the man," Hanks said. He appeared to be approaching sixty, but he was tall and slim, having kept himself in condition over the years. "What's your business in Yankton?"

"I'm here for the McCall trial."

"The real one, this time?"

"Right."

"Did you know Hickok?"

Clint nodded. "Old friends."

"Rough, having a man like that die that way," Hanks said. "It's indecent."

"My feelings exactly."

"Can I do something for you while you're here?"

"I like to check in with the law in every town I visit," Clint explained. "Sometimes it saves on trouble later on."

"Smart move."

"You could tell me when McCall's trial is slated to start, though."

"Day after tomorrow. Seems the judge is anxious to right any wrongs that might have been done by that miner's court in Deadwood."

"Is there any doubt in anyone's mind that he killed Hickok?" Clint asked.

"The lawman who arrested him said he was bragging on it, but you can never tell with juries. I've seen some pretty strange verdicts handed down."

"I guess we'll just have to wait and see," Clint said. "Marshal, would you mind telling me where you're holding McCall?"

"Right here," Hanks said, jerking his head towards a door behind him. "I've got him in the back."

Just as Clint was trying to think of a good reason Hanks should let him see McCall, the marshal said, "Do you want to get a look at him?"

"I don't mind if I do, Marshal. Thanks."

"This way," the laid-back lawman said. He grabbed his keys, opened the door to the main cell block, and then led the way through the door to the proper cell.

"That's your man," he said, indicating the man in the cell.

Clint look at McCall and felt the rage build up inside of him. How could Bill allow such an insignificant-looking individual to end his life?"

"Who are you?" McCall demanded, looking up at Clint from his cot.

"A man who came to see you hang, McCall."

"I ain't gonna hang, friend," McCall sneered.

"You're going to pay, *friend,*" Clint told him, "one way or another, you're going to pay."

Hank, sensing Adams's mood, stepped in and said, "See you in court, McCall. Let's go, Mr. Adams."

Clint kept his eyes on McCall a few moments longer, burning the man's scruffy features into his mind, and then relented and followed the marshal out.

"Much obliged for your time and trouble, Marshal," Clint said.

"No trouble," Hanks said. "Come over to the Yankton House saloon later and I'll buy you a beer."

"I just might take you up on that, Marshal," The Gunsmith said, and left.

Marshal Hanks stared at the closed door for a few moments, wondering if he was going to have any trouble from the infamous Gunsmith. The man definitely had something eating at his insides, and the lawman had a feeling it was more than just the death of a good friend.

"Hey, Marshal!" McCall's voice called from the cell block.

Hanks sighed, picked up his keys and went back to see what his prisoner wanted.

"What do you want, McCall?"

McCall got up off his cot and came over to the front of the cell. Pushing his face up against the bars he asked, "Who was that guy, anyway. What the hell did he want?"

"That was a friend of Bill Hickok, McCall," Hanks told him, "and he just wanted to get a good look at you, that's all."

"What for?"

"I guess he just wanted to make sure he'd remember you, if he ever saw you again."

"Who was he?" McCall asked. "What's his name?"

"If I tell you you're just gonna lose sleep worrying about it," Hanks said.

"Damn it—"

"All right," Hanks said. "I warned you. His name is Clint Adams."

"So?"

"Some people call him the Gunsmith."

McCall said, "Wha—" and his eyes popped.

"Pleasant dreams."

THIRTEEN

Clint found Colorado Charlie Utter seated at a back table. He had his back to the door and had left Clint the seat against the wall. He bought a beer and went over and joined Charlie.

Clint sipped his beer, and eyed the one Charlie had in front of him with suspicion. The level was too high for it to be the man's first, even if he'd been nursing it. Still, if the man wanted to drink, there was really nothing he'd be able to do about it.

"You saw McCall?"

"I did."

"So now that you know what he looks like, you don't need me anymore, is that it?"

"That's right," Clint said. "You're on your own again, Charlie."

Charlie looked at his three-quarters full mug of

beer, and then pushed it away, saying, "Maybe I'll just stick around until after the trial."

"I can't keep paying your expenses."

Utter waved that away and said, "I'll make do. I always have." He stood up and said to Clint, "I'll be around, Clint, if you should need a hand."

"I'll remember, Charlie," he said. "Thanks."

Probably in another saloon, Clint thought, and then he thought that maybe he wasn't being fair.

As he was lifting his own beer to his lips he saw the batwing doors swing open and Charlie Utter walked in again. He put the beer down as Charlie walked up to the table and sat back down again.

"I thought you might be interested in something I just saw," Colorado Charlie said.

"What's that?"

"I just seen Tim Brady walking down the street, and where Brady is, Varnes can't be too far behind."

"Brady and Varnes," Clint repeated. The two men who might have put McCall up to killing Hickok— only it wasn't "might have" anymore. Why else would they be in Yankton if it wasn't to make sure that McCall didn't talk?

"Did you follow him?"

Charlie shook his head. "He knows me. Both him and Varnes know me—but they don't know you."

"And I don't know them," Clint added, "so I guess we still need each other after all, don't we, Charlie?"

"I guess so," Charlie said, "but that don't mean you have to keep paying my way. I'll make do."

"If you say so," Clint said, "but let me know where you'll be staying so we can stay in touch."

"Sure, Clint."

As Charlie started to get up, Clint looked at the

beer on the table and said, "It's a shame to let that go to waste."

"That's okay, Clint," Charlie said. "We still got a job to do, for Bill."

Staring at Charlie, Clint put his own beer down next to the one on the table and said, "You're absolutely right, Charlie."

"I'll see you later, Clint."

"Right, Charlie."

Charlie left again, and Clint leaned back in his chair and eyed the two beers on the table. Colorado Charlie Utter was absolutely right. They still had a job to do for Wild Bill Hickok. McCall was first, and then it would be Varnes's and Brady's turn.

Of course, they could have just let Varnes and Brady kill McCall, but Clint wanted McCall to hang, legally, for the murder of Hickok. If he was acquitted, however—well, there were other ways of making sure justice was served.

Hickok always had his own idea about justice, and although they were friends, Clint didn't always agree with Bill's way of doing things, but if McCall should be set free again, through some fluke—or bribe— Clint hoped that he'd be up to making McCall pay, with Wild Bill's brand of justice, the justice he'd brought to Hays City and Abilene.

The problem with Bill's justice was that it backfired sometimes—as it had eventually in Hays City and in Abilene—but if Clint decided that Bill's justice was what he needed, he was going to make damn sure it worked.

FOURTEEN

When Clint saw the girl, he realized that it had
been a long time since he'd had a woman. The saloon
was not very busy, and she was just standing at the
bar, talking with the bartender. She was wearing a
sequined dress that exposed her shoulders and the
beginning slopes of her breasts. Her hair was dark
and pinned behind her head, but he thought that, un-
pinned, it would probably fall well down her back.
Her breasts were full, her waist slim, and he judged
her to be about twenty-five. She looked over towards
him at that point and caught him examining her. Her
gaze held his, and then she said something to the
bartender and began to walk over to his table.

"Hello there," she said.

"Hi."

"Your eyes like to burned holes in me, the way

you was staring," she told him. "Been a while since
you been with a girl?"

"A while," he said.

"Would you like to go on upstairs and get to know
each other a little better?"

"What's your name?"

"Billie, with a *i-e*." She had her hands on her hips
and her chest thrust out as she posed for him.

"Well, Billie, I tell you, it might be a while since
I've been with a lady, but it hasn't been so long that
I'll start paying for my pleasure."

"You don't pay, huh?"

"Never have, never will."

She studied him for a few moments now, then
looked around the saloon. There were two other girls
moving among the customers, one a blonde and the
other a redhead, but the place was still slow and they
were mostly sitting in a lap or just watching a poker
game.

"I tell *you* what," Billie said. "It ain't busy down
here, and it won't get busy for a while, so why don't
we just go upstairs and get better acquainted."

"On the house?" he asked, showing his surprise.

"That's right," she said. "What's the matter, don't
you think I ever do it just for fun, or just for the hell
of it? What do you say?"

Her eyes were bold as they held his, and he felt
the heat rising in his groin.

"My name is Clint," he said.

"Pleased to meet you, Clint," she said with a mock
curtsy. "You gonna leave me standing here all shame-
less, or are you gonna take me upstairs?"

"You got it backwards, Billie," he said, standing
up. "You're going to take me upstairs."

"Well, just so long as we go," she said. She took

his hand and led him to the stairs, where he followed her up to the second floor.

"This is my room," she said. For a moment, Clint wondered if she wasn't trying to set him up for some male partner to rob him. He'd never run across a saloon girl—or whore—who was so eager to give it away, but then he guessed that maybe they did do it once in a while just for the hell of it.

"Coming in?" she asked. She had crossed the threshold into her room and he had still been standing in the hall. "I swear, if I didn't know any better—and I don't, come to think of it—I'd think this was your first time, honey."

"Not the first time," he said, entering her room, "not by a longshot, but the first time since—"

"Since when?" she asked when he stopped short.

"Since I was . . . in Texas, which was a while back."

"Well, honey," she said, slipping the straps of her dress off her shoulders, "little Billie is gonna make it worth the wait, you just wait and see."

Actually, she wasn't all that little. As she slipped the top of her dress down, her bountiful breasts bobbed into view, lushly plump and topped with coppery nipples. She slid the dress down to her ankles and discarded it, then removed her stockings and underthings, until she was standing there with her hands on her hips, posing again.

"How do you like me?" she asked.

"I like you just fine, Billie," he said, his eyes taking in the wiry black bush between her legs. "Just fine."

It *had* been a while since his last woman—before Bill's death and before his slow descent into the bottle—and he felt his erection painfully constricted inside his pants.

"You just stand there and let me look at you while

I get undressed," he told her.

"Oh, no," she replied. "I'll help you undress."

She stepped forward and worked on the buttons of his shirt, until she was able to peel it off him, then her hands dropped to his belt and pants and then she was tugging them down to his ankles. She had to take off his boots before she could discard the pants, and then his underthings quickly followed, and they were naked together.

"Mmm," she said. "It has been a long time, hasn't it. That thing looks like it's going to pop anytime now."

She dropped to her knees in front of him and gently cupped his scrotum. She rolled his balls around in her hand, then took hold of the base of his penis and began to rub it against her breasts. Grasping one plump breast in each hand she closed them around his penis, trapping the hot, pulsating column of flesh in the valley between them, and she gently began to roll it back and forth while she kissed his belly, and stuck her tongue into his navel.

Abruptly, she put her hands behind him, cupping his buttocks, and began to grind her chest against his groin, licking his belly. She abandoned that only long enough to reach higher with her tongue and lick his nipples until they were hard little points, then she went back down, held his penis in her hand and started licking the swollen head. Clint groaned and was afraid he would shoot there and then, but she slid her hand to the base of his cock and squeezed, quelling his desire to come, but not lessening the pleasure he felt as her tongue swiped back and forth over the head.

"Mmm," she said again, and then opened her mouth and took him inside.

"Jesus . . ." he moaned. His hands moved to the

back of her head, holding her there while she suckled his penis, still holding him so that he couldn't come. He pulled the pins from her hair and allowed her dark tresses to tumble down her back.

"Oh, mister," she moaned, letting him slide from her mouth so that she could lick the length of him, "you taste so good."

"Well, let's see if I can say the same for you," he said. He put his hands under her arms and pulled her to her feet, then deposited her on the bed. He was on her quickly, sucking her nipples and breasts for all he was worth, while his fingers worked between her legs.

She cupped the back of his head in her hands, holding him against her breasts. Her hips came up to meet the pressure of his fingers as her cries became louder and louder.

"Now," he said, freeing her breasts, "we'll see."

He slid down until his face was nestled between her legs, and he was happy to find that she tasted just fine. His tongue lapped at the folds of her cunt, and then, using his teeth and lips, he found that tiny nub and began sucking on it. She bounced and writhed beneath him as he held her down tightly, and finally she screamed, "Oh, God!" as her body was racked by the spasms of her pleasure.

He climbed atop her before her spasms were complete and drove himself into her, causing her mouth to open wide and the cords on her neck to stand out.

"Jesus!" she cried out, whipping her head from side to side while he continued to take her in long, hard strokes. Finally, her legs came up to encircle his waist, and he felt her muscles contract around his swollen organ as she literally milked his seed from him while she experienced another spasm of delight.

"God, Clint," she said, still holding him tightly around the waist with her powerful legs, "maybe I should be paying you!"

A few hours later, Clint left Billie in her room and went down to the saloon to have a beer. The time spent with her had had a very therapeutic effect on him. It was as if he had gotten rid of a lot of that pent-up emotion he'd been keeping locked inside of him.

Some of it . . . but not all.

After the one beer he left the saloon and went in search of a newspaper office. A city this size had to have more than one, but one was all he needed— preferably the biggest one, one that would have back copies of not only their own paper, but other large papers, as well.

After asking directions, he finally reached the offices of the Yankton *Star*.

He entered the office and saw that there were several employees working there, but one in particular caught his eye. She was a pretty little thing of about eighteen, with long brown hair and large brown eyes. She was wearing a man's shirt that was several sizes too large for her, and also a printer's apron.

Wiping her hands on the apron, she approached him and asked, "Can I help you, mister?"

If she knew how attractive she was, it didn't show in her eyes, or in her manner. Her gaze was open and innocent.

"I'd like to talk to the editor, if I can," he said.

"That'd be my grandfather, but he's not here right now."

"What's his name?"

"Amos Walker."

"And your name?"

"Amy," she said. "Named after him, close as they

could get it."

"When will he be back, Amy?"

She shrugged.

"Depends on whether he went to the café or a saloon. Could be any minute, could be a few hours. Is there something I can help you with?"

"I'd like to get a look at some back issues of your newspaper," he said. "Do I need an okay from him for that?"

"Naw, I can take care of that. What issues?"

"I don't know specific dates, but anything that has to do with the Wild Bill Hickok killing."

"Oh, that?" she said. "We had a few issues on that. I can find them for you."

"Hold on a minute," he said as she started to walk away. "I'd also like back issues of any other major newspapers that you might have."

"Also about Mr. Hickok?" she asked.

"That's right."

"Take me a little longer to put all of that together for you."

"Can you do it? I'd be very grateful."

"I wouldn't expect any payment, mister. I can have it put together for you by later this evening. Can you come by about seven?"

"I could do that, sure," he said. "I'd be much obliged, Amy."

"No problem. Didn't you read all all that stuff when it first happened, though?"

"Uh, no, I was sick, and I wasn't able to read any newspapers," he explained.

"Oh. Well, I'll have them got together by seven, Mr. . . . ."

"Adams, Clint Adams," he said. "I'd also be much obliged if you would let me buy you some dinner later on, as a gesture of thanks."

She cocked her head to one side, examining him in detail, and then said, "I guess there's no harm in that."

"Fine, then I'll pick you, and the papers, up at seven o'clock sharp."

"We'll be ready, Clint," she said. "I got to get back to work now. If Gramps went to a saloon, I'll have to get out the evening edition for him."

"That's a big job."

She smiled and said, "I been doing it since I was twelve years old."

Clint smiled back and said, "I'll see you later, Amy."

"'Bye, Clint."

She went back to work, and Clint backed towards the door, watching her move about, a bundle of energy with not a bit wasted. She handled the big press with ease and gave orders to the other two workers—a boy her own age and a man in his fifties—as if she had indeed been doing it for years.

More relaxed than he had been in weeks, Clint found himself looking forward to picking up those papers later that evening.

FIFTEEN

The Yankton House Saloon was packed with people drinking and gambling and doing whatever else people do in a big city saloon. Feeling pretty good after his session with Billie and the promise of dinner with Amy, Clint shouldered his way to the bar and ordered a beer. While waiting for it, he looked around for the marshal, but apparently he had not yet arrived. When his beer came he started to lift it to his mouth and caught a glimpse of himself in the bar mirror.

His face had filled out some, to a point where he almost looked normal again. His deep chest had also filled in again, as had his shoulders. All in all, he felt damned good, almost completely recovered from his suicidal drinking binge.

Still, there was that something still buried deep inside of him, waiting for him to take it out and examine it closely—when he was ready. . . .

"You pay for that yet?" a voice asked, followed by a hand clapping him on the shoulder.

Jarred from his thoughts, he turned and found Marshal Hanks standing next to him.

"Uh, no, I haven't paid yet," Clint replied.

"Good," the lawman replied. "Jason, bring me a beer and put both of these on my tab," he called out to the bartender.

"Thanks, Marshal."

"Just keeping my promise," Hanks said, accepting his beer from Jason. "Cheers," he said, and they both drank. "What have you been up to?"

"Just keeping myself occupied," Clint said, "taking a look at Yankton."

"What do you think?"

"Pretty impressive."

"Yeah, and it's still growing. Lots of people coming in, especially now for the trial."

"I expect that will be something of an event," Clint commented.

"Oh, yes. Already, there are reporters here from several large out-of-town newspapers."

"Uh-huh," Clint said. "I met someone from the Yankton *Star* today."

"Amos Walker?"

"No, his granddaughter, Amy."

"Ah, a pretty young thing, that one," Hanks said. "If I were twenty or thirty years younger..." He trailed off and looked about the room. "There's Amos now, with his nose in a bottle."

Clint looked in the direction the lawman indicated, and saw a man about Hank's age, with disheveled white hair and a large, bulbous nose, which was indeed just about stuck down the neck of a bottle of whiskey.

"Does he do that often?"

"About half the time," Hanks said. "The other half he's a damned decent newspaperman."

"Have you know him long?"

"Ha, I've known Amos for over thirty years," Hanks said.

"What makes him drink like that?"

Hanks shrugged and turned to face the bar again.

"Gettin' old, I reckon," he said. "That and the death of his wife, more than six years ago." A faraway look crept into the lawman's eyes as he spoke of Amos Walker's wife.

"How did she die?"

"Pneumonia."

"Did you know her, as well?"

"Know her?" he replied. "I loved her almost as much as he did, thirty years ago. Amy could have been my granddaughter."

"What happened?"

Hanks looked at Clint, and said, "What happens when you pin on a badge, Clint? You should know, you wore one long enough."

Clint remembered a girl he had lost because of his badge, and nodded.

"I know."

"So he got the girl, and I got my badge. Then it was a deputy sheriff's badge, then a sheriff, now a U.S. federal marshal." He turned again to look at his old friend. "I've got to make my rounds, Clint. Do me a favor, will you? See that he gets home all right?"

"Where's home?"

"Right above the *Star* offices."

"No problem, then. I've got to go back there at seven."

"Oh? What for?"

"To pick up some back newspapers and to take Amy to dinner," Clint said.

Hanks's face went stony for a moment, and then he said, "Remember what I said about Amy, Clint. She could have been my granddaughter."

Clint looked into the old lawman's eyes, and then replied, "I'll remember, Marshal."

Hanks nodded, then repeated, "Watch Amos for me, will you? Sometimes he gets so bad he can't find his way home. He's ended up in a horse trough more than once."

"Don't worry."

"Much obliged." He spoke to the bartender, and then told Clint, "You can drink your fill on my tab."

"Thanks," Clint said, raising his mug, "but this will be enough."

Hanks nodded to the Gunsmith, and left.

Clint rested his elbows on the bar top and continued to nurse his solitary beer—his second of the day, as he was well aware. Using the mirror, he kept his eyes on Amy's grandfather, who continued to suck on his whiskey bottle until it was empty. At that point he began to search through his pockets, and from his manner it became obvious that he didn't have the money for another.

"Hey, Grandpa," a voice called from another table. "You need another drink?"

Both Amos Walker and Clint Adams sought out the speaker, and found him at the very next table. He was a big, sandy-haired man, unshaven, sitting with a saloon girl in his substantial lap. He had a black patch over one eye and a scar down that same side of his face—the right—which stopped at his lip, causing it to curl just a bit at the corner.

"Don't give the old fool any of my whiskey," a

second man at the table growled. He was of a comparable size to the first man, dark-haired, with a large, walrus mustache and thick-fingered hands. Both men were dressed in dusty trail clothes, with well-worn hats resting on the table. He couldn't see their guns, but he had no doubt that they would also be well worn and ill kept. These were no gunhawks, but brawlers, and it seemed as if they were about to brawl with each other.

"He needs a drink, the old man does," the black-patched man said. "Besides, he reminds me of my own father."

"You don't know who your father was," the second man shot back, "and neither does your mother."

Instead of taking offense, the man with the patch leaned his head back and let out a hearty bellow of laughter, saying, "By God, you're right about that!" He laughed further, and when the laughter had faded he said, "Still, I think I'll give him a drink," and reached for the solitary bottle on the table.

"Not from my bottle," the second man said, pulling the bottle away before the first man could touch it.

"Buckman," the first man said, "I want that old man to have a drink."

Buckman stared at the man with the patch, then put the bottle down and said, "I'm not going to fight with you over an old man neither one of us knows, Hedge."

The man with the patch took that as a surrender on Buckman's part, which was a mistake. As he started to pour the old man a drink. Buckman stood up and walked to Amos Walker's table.

"Get out, old man," he said. "If you don't have the money for a drink, get out."

Walker did not talk back. He began to get to his

feet but was unsteady and fell back into the chair.

"Get up and get out, I said!" bellowed the man called Buckman. He dropped one thick-fingered paw onto Walker's shoulder, and Clint saw the old man wince with pain.

"Buckman," the man with the patch called, but before he could slide out from beneath the girl in his lap, Clint put down his beer mug and approached the tableau at the old man's table.

"Take your hand off him, Buckman," Clint said tightly.

"Eh?" Buckman said, looking at Clint. The Gunsmith was tall, but his musculature was deceptive. The breadth of his shoulders and chest could not be seen when he was dressed, and he seemed much slimmer than he actually was.

"Get lost, before I bend you in half," the big man told him.

Buckman turned back to the seated Amos Walker, but Clint spoke up again.

"I said move your hand, you big oaf!" Clint snapped.

"You better do what the man says, Buckman," Hedge spoke up. He had been watching Clint and had seen something Buckman had not. His advice to his friend was sincere—not that Buckman would take it. He was a man who had to learn things the hard way.

"Does he remind you of your father too?" Buckman asked.

"It doesn't matter whose father he is," Clint said. "He has a right to sit where he pleases."

"He was gonna drink my whiskey," Buckman snarled.

"He hadn't made a move to drink anyone's whiskey," Clint replied, "and if I heard correctly, your friend was the one offering him a drink."

"From my bottle!"

Clint fished a coin out of his pocket and said, "Did you pay for the bottle?"

"Yeah!"

Flipping the coin to the big man, who grabbed for it and missed, Clint said, "Now it's my bottle, and I say anyone can drink from it, if he wants to."

"I don't want to," Walker said, speaking for the first time. "I can buy my own whiskey."

He shrugged off Buckman's hand, which had lessened its grip until it was merely lying on the old man's shoulder.

Buckman lifted his arm, as if to backhand the old man across the face, but Clint stepped in and caught the big man's wrist in his own hand.

"Mister, you're asking for a beating," Buckman snarled, his boozy breath assailing the Gunsmith's nostrils.

"And you're asking for a lesson in manners," Clint replied.

"And you're both asking for trouble!" a third voice shouted, from the entrance to the saloon.

Both men turned to see Marshal Hanks. The gray-haired lawman was standing with his legs spread and his hand resting on the butt of his gun.

"You're both visitors to this town," he went on, "and as such you'll abide by the laws, or leave. I don't want any brawling in here. You want to fight, take it outside the city limits. Understood?"

Buckman pulled his arm free of Clint's grip and, muttering, he returned to his table, where Hedge greeted him with laughter.

Hanks approached Clint and said, "I'll take Amos home."

"I can do it. Why don't you continue your rounds."

Hanks looked at his old friend, then he told Clint, "All right. I'll check on him later."

"I'll tell him," Clint said.

Hanks turned and cast a glance at Buckman, who was still muttering under his breath while his friend chuckled, and then walked out again.

"Mr. Walker," Clint said, leaning over the old man. "Amy sent me to take you home."

"Amy?" the old man asked, looking up at Clint.

"She's worried about you," Clint said, taking the old man by the arm.

"Little Amy," the old man said, allowing Clint to bring him to his feet, "as sweet as her mother was."

Clint took hold of the old man's shoulders and began steering him towards the door.

"Hey, friend," Buckman's voice called out.

Clint turned his head so he could look at the big man. His friend, Hedge, seemed to be trying to keep him from speaking, but Buckman shook his friend off and directed his attention to Clint.

"We ain't finished yet, friend."

"Any time, *friend,*" Clint replied, and walked Amos Walker through the batwing doors and on home.

SIXTEEN

"You're early," Amy Walker said when Clint opened the door to the *Star* offices, but then she saw her grandfather as Clint led him in. "Oh," she said, "Gramps. Again?"

"Again," her grandfather said. "Still, what's the difference?" The old man put his hand to his head and said, "I'm tired."

"David," she said, calling to the youth who appeared to be her own age, or perhaps a year older.

"Yes, Amy?" the boy asked.

"Would you take my grandfather upstairs and put him to bed, please?" she asked.

"Of course," the boy said, and Clint could see his eyes shine as he spoke to the girl.

When David had taken her grandfather upstairs, Clint said, "That boy, David. He's in love with you."

"Oh, I know that," she said, turning her attention

to the press again. "I've got one more page to do,
Clint, then I'll clean up and we'll go to dinner. You
can tell me then how you came to bring Gramps home."

"I'll wait."

"While you wait, you might want to look through
those papers I collected for you," she said. Using her
ink-stained chin to point she indicated the stack of
papers on a chair beneath the window.

"I'll just be a few minutes," she added.

"Don't rush."

Clint walked to the stack of papers, which was
about six inches thick, and decided that he would be
better off leaving them for later in his room.

He turned and decided that he'd rather watch Amy
work, which she did with total concentration. It was
not until she had satisfactorily finished her task that
she looked up at him again and found him staring at
her.

"What are you staring at?" she asked, smiling self-
consciously.

"Just a pretty lady," he said, "with ink smudges
all over her face."

Her hands flew to her face, promptly adding still
another ink smudge.

"I must look a fright," she said. "Clint, I wonder..."

"You want more time?"

"Just to clean up thoroughly, and maybe to look
in on my grandfather. Would you mind awfully if I
took another half an hour?"

"No, I don't mind," he said. "I can use the time
to bring these papers up to my room, and clean up a
little myself." He picked up the bundle and said, "I'll
see you in a half hour."

"Thank you for understanding."

"What's to understand?" he said. "Take your time, and don't forget the smudge right on the tip of your pretty nose."

He left her touching her nose, and headed for his hotel.

Forty minutes later Clint was seated at a table in the café with what he considered to be the prettiest girl in town—possibly the prettiest he'd ever seen. Oh, he'd been with woman who were more beautiful, or sexier, but not who'd been so damned pretty, like a newborn filly.

And he told her so, several times.

Over dinner she said, "If you keep complimenting me, and looking at me like that, you're going to make my face permanently red from blushing."

"Either that, or you'll learn not to blush," he replied.

"Maybe," she said. "Clint, Gramps told me what you did for him in the saloon. I'm grateful."

"That's all right," I said. "The marshal had asked me to look out for him, anyway."

"Uncle Jeff," she said warmly. "He's a dear man. He's been like a second grandfather to me."

"What happened to your parents, Amy?"

She lowered her eyes and said, "They both died." She didn't elaborate, so Clint didn't pursue it.

"Did those newspapers help you?" she asked.

"Some," he said. Fact of the matter was, he barely had time to look at them. He figured to do that later on. He'd taken a bath and changed his clothes during that extra half hour, wanting to look decent if he was going to be seen in public with a filly like Amy.

"Why are you so interested in seeing old newspapers?" she asked. "Are you here for the trial?"

"The answer to both of those questions is yes," he

said, smiling. "Bill Hickok was a good friend of mine. I'm interested in the facts surrounding his death."

"Yet you didn't read them when they first came out?" she asked. "Oh, that's right, you said you were sick."

"That's not exactly true, Amy," he said. "Actually, I started to drink pretty bad when I heard about Bill. I was too drunk to read those newspapers then, but I'm sober enough to read them now."

"I'm sorry," she apologized. "It must have been very hard for you." She leaned forward and added, "I'm only asking you this because of Gramps. You can see he drinks, and I was wondering—well, what was it that made you stop drinking?"

"Well, I wasn't doing it for as long as your grandfather has, but when I found out that Bill's killer had gone free, it kind of sobered me right up. I took some time to get back on my feet, and here I am."

"To see that it doesn't happen again?" she asked, and then she went on quickly, before he could respond. "I'm sorry, Clint. I had no right to say that. It's just that I know who you are—"

"I'm Clint Adams," he said. "I'm a man, like any other man."

"Like Bill Hickok was a man?" she asked. "Like Wes Hardin?"

"I'm not like them," Clint said. "I was Bill's friend, but I wasn't like him."

"No, you're not like them," she agreed, "but people think you are, because they know you as the Gunsmith. A few moments ago, I asked you a question, which was prompted by the fact that I knew you were the Gunsmith, and I apologize again."

Clint looked at her, sitting there so serious, and he

smiled at her and said, "We're getting too serious here, Amy."

"I just want you to know that now, when I look at you, I see Clint Adams, and that's all."

"I appreciate that," he said. "I truly do."

After dinner Clint walked Amy home.

"Do you want me to come in with you while you check on your grandfather?" he asked. "You might need some help with him."

"Oh, I've been handling Gramps ever since—ever since Grandma died."

"Your mother was his daughter?"

"Yes."

"I understand you came close to being Marshal Hanks's granddaughter."

She smiled and said, "That's what I heard from Grandma. She said she loved Grandpa and Uncle Jeff the same, only Uncle Jeff loved the law more than he did her, so he made the decision for her."

"Did she ever regret it?"

"Not once, I don't think," she said. "In a way, she still had both of them, it's just that Grandpa was the one she lived with."

"And had children with."

"Yes," she said. "My mother. Uncle Jeff loved her like she was his own daughter."

"And he loves you too," Clint said. "Just that much."

"I know," she said. "I should go up now, Clint. Thank you for a lovely dinner."

"Maybe we could do it again while I'm in town," Clint said.

She touched his right arm and said, "I'd like that very much, Clint. Good night."

"Good night, Amy."

Clint went back to his room then and began leafing through the newspapers that Amy Walker had provided for him. He read carefully all the accounts of Bill Hickok's death—his murder—and the subsequent accounts of Jack McCall's trial in Deadwood. He became convinced that anyone reading the facts of the case as printed in the papers could only come to one decision, and that was that Jack McCall had shot and killed Bill Hickok from behind in cold blood.

Yet McCall had gone free.

It was encouraging that a court of law had found it necessary to negate the ruling of the Deadwood "miner's court" and try Jack McCall again, but there was no guarantee that he wouldn't be set free again.

Amy had been right, of course. He was here to make sure McCall didn't get off free again, whether the court acquitted him or not. Had she been right, then, in saying that she didn't believe that he was like Hickok or Hardin? Wouldn't that be up to him to prove or disprove? She was also right about people judging him by his reputation as the Gunsmith. He didn't like the name, had never liked it, yet he had never publicly disavowed it either, and it was much too late in life to do that.

If Jack McCall got off again, and Clint killed him, wouldn't he then be proving that he was deserving of the reputation that had followed him around for most of his life?

Still, Bill was his friend, and he wouldn't be able to stand by idly while his killer went free.

He would just have to watch the trial very carefully, and hope that McCall was found guilty.

SEVENTEEN

The next morning Clint had breakfast in the hotel dining room. Over breakfast he wondered what had become of Colorado Charlie. Had he found a place to sleep? He wished he could afford to continue paying Charlie's expenses, but the simple fact of the matter was that his funds were running low. In the past he'd been able to pick up money repairing guns, but his rig was in Wyoming. If his money ran out while he was in Yankton, he was going to be in a bind. He hoped that wouldn't happen, at least until the trial was over.

When he was working on his second pot of good, strong coffee, the marshal came into the dining room and approached his table.

"'Morning, Marshal."

"Good morning, Mr. Adams," Hanks replied.

"Sit down, Marshal. Have a cup of coffee. And

call me Clint. Being called 'mister' by a lawman always makes me think I'm suspected of something."

"I don't suspect you of anything, Clint," Hanks said, sitting down. A waiter appeared with another cup, and Hanks poured himself a cup of coffee.

"Well, that's good," Clint said. "To what do I owe this early morning visit, then?"

"I just wanted to thank you for what you did for Amos Walker last night."

"Don't worry about it," Clint said, even though he had the feeling there was more than that on the lawman's mind. "What else, Marshal?"

Hanks sipped his coffee, then put the cup down and stared at Clint across the table with troubled eyes.

"I hear you had dinner with Amy Walker last night," he said.

"Yeah, well I told you last night that I was going to have dinner with her."

"That's right, you did," Hanks said.

"After dinner I walked her home."

"That was decent of you," the marshal said. "She's a good girl, Clint. I wouldn't take kindly to seeing her get hurt."

"Neither would I, Marshal," Clint said. "And I wouldn't have any reason to hurt her."

"I guess I'm just a worrier when it comes to her," Hanks said.

For the first time Clint noticed how tired Hanks looked, and older than he'd originally guessed. He now put the man's age at over sixty. He was probably the same age as Amos Walker, although Walker looked like a man who was over seventy.

"She get Amos into bed okay?" the lawman asked.

"Yeah, she had some kid—uh, David—take him upstairs, and then she went up to check on him."

"David, yeah, the kid's been working for Amos for about six months now."

"He seems to be in love with Amy, or something," Clint said.

He grinned and said, "Yeah, but she don't even know the kid's alive, except to give him orders at the paper."

"I noticed that," Clint said. He finished his coffee and shook the pot, finding it empty. "I guess that's it, unless you want some more coffee?"

"No, not for me, thanks," the marshal said. I've got to get to work."

"Who's with McCall at the jail?" Clint asked.

"I've got four deputies, Clint, although you haven't met any of them yet. Someone is always there with him."

Clint called over the waiter and paid his bill.

"What do you have planned for today?" Hanks asked as they walked out.

"Nothing, really. I guess I've just got to keep myself amused until the trial starts. Maybe I'll go looking for my friend."

"Your friend?"

They were outside on the boardwalk in front of the hotel now, and Clint could see that the town was wide awake. The streets were crowded with people going about their business.

"Yeah, he rode into town with me. Name's Charlie Utter. He's also a friend of—*was* a friend of Hickok's."

"I see. I hope he's as content as you are to wait for the outcome of the trial."

"He is."

"Clint, what are your plans if McCall is acquitted again?" Hanks asked.

Clint hesitated a moment, then admitted, "I don't rightly know, Marshal."

"I hope we don't end up bumping heads over this," Hanks said. "I'm a little long in the tooth for that kind of thing."

"I'm sure we both want as little trouble as possible, Marshal."

EIGHTEEN

Clint starting checking out the cheaper hotels and boardinghouses in town for Colorado Charlie Utter. When he failed to find him, he starting checking out stables and barns, and finally found out where Charlie had spent the night.

"Yep," the owner of one stable said, "I let a feller fittin' that description sleep in my barn last night."

"Did you charge him?"

"I would have," the man said, "if he'd had any money. Town's filling up pretty quick for the trial tomorrow."

"Did he say where he was going this morning?"

"Said he was gonna go looking for some breakfast." The man, who was in his mid-fifties and looked every hard-spent year of it, said, "I couldn't very well give him that for nothing, could I?"

"Well, I guess not," Clint said. "Thanks." He took

out ten dollars and gave it to the man, saying, "If he comes back, let him spend the night again, and give him something to eat, will you?"

"Well, sure," the man said, eyeing the money in his hand. "Whatever you say, mister."

"If we're in town for a long period of time, I'll come back and give you some more money."

"That's fine with me," the man said.

"Just don't let my friend know I'm paying you."

"What if your friend wants to know how come I'm all of a sudden feeding him?"

"Just tell him you're doing it out of the goodness of your heart."

"By golly, I'll do that," the man said, beaming. "The goodness of my heart. I like that!"

"Sure you do," Clint said, "as long as you get paid for it."

Clint left Charlie Utter's new home to walk to the livery stable where he'd left Duke and to check on the big fella. Maybe he'd even take him out for some exercise.

He wasn't in the best part of Yankton, and now he was picking his way back to a main street through back alleys. It never occurred to him that he might have been followed . . . until the first shot.

The bullet went by him before he even heard the sound of it and imbedded itself in the wall of a building to his right. Clint threw himself to the dirt, rolling, and automatically pulled his gun at the same time. He came to a stop with his back to the wall, and when another bullet struck the wall next to his head he began to run along the wall towards one end of the alley, making himself as small a target as possible.

There was one more shot before he reached the end of the alley, and then he was able to take refuge underneath a stairway and attempt to see where the shots were coming from.

He waited beneath the steps to see if the shooter would try to follow him. To do that, however, the person would have to expose himself in that alley, the way Clint had just been exposed, and he doubted that would happen.

He waited a few moments longer, but when he became convinced that the shooter was gone, he moved out from beneath the stairs to see if he was right. When there were no shots, he decided to chance it and go back through the alley to the other end, even though it would mean once again leaving himself vulnerable.

He stepped into the alley as if the floor of it were filled with rattlesnakes, ready to jump back at the first hint of venom.

Keeping close to the right wall, he traveled the length of the alley, then slipped around the corner with his gun out, finally determining that the shooter had gone.

Walking back through the alley without incident, he continued on, finally coming out onto a main street, where he holstered his gun. In relative safety, he was now able to address the question of who had been shooting at him.

He chose the Yankton House as the place to do it, over a beer.

"A little early, isn't it?" the bartender asked good-naturedly.

"You're absolutely right," Clint replied, and took his beer to a corner table.

Clint had been shot at enough times in his life to know that simply being there was reason enough. Somebody had recognized him by his rep and taken a potshot at him in an attempt to make a name for himself—like Jack McCall. Maybe somebody who was in town for the trial had gotten liquored up and decided to rid the West of another of its legends.

That was just naturally the first reason that came into the Gunsmith's mind every time he was shot at—and if he had a nickel for every time he was shot at, he'd buy himself a nice little town somewhere and cut himself off from the rest of the so-called civilized world.

Why bother to even wonder? he told himself. He'd played this scene so many times before. There were times when he never found out who had shot at him, or why.

What a hell of a way to live, accepting the fact that you are a walking or—as in the case of Bill Hickok—a sitting target for any coward with a gun.

The incident had served to fire his eagerness for McCall's trial to begin—and, unfortunately, it had also fired his thirst.

NINETEEN

Something that felt like it had fur and eight legs was crawling around inside his mouth, and it wasn't until he tried to spit it out that he realized it was his own tongue.

His eyes felt gritty and sticky at the same time and he had to try several times before he succeeded in opening them. The ceiling looked first as if it were at the end of his nose and then as if it were miles away. He waited for it to make up its mind and stop halfway between before he attempted to examine his surroundings.

He appeared to be in his own hotel room, and there was someone with him, although they were out of eye range at the moment. He heard what sounded like water dripping, and then something cold and damp landed on his forehead while he was looking at the window. He brought his eyes back to the ceiling, but there was a face blocking his way now, and a very pretty face it was.

It was Amy Walker.

"You're awake," she said. She took the damp rag from his forehead and used it to clean his eyes for him, although he couldn't determine any noticeable difference. She replaced the rag on his forehead and smiled at him.

His head was pounding now and his symptoms began to make some sense to him. Immediately following Bill's death he had awakened on many a morning-after feeling just this way.

"Oh, God," he said, as he realized what had happened.

"Clint," she said, not quite understanding his reaction, "you drank a little too much, that's all."

"I slid back," he replied. "What day is it, Amy?"

"You've only been here since early this morning, Clint. The trial starts today. You haven't missed anything."

"Thank God for that," he said, moving to sit up.

"You'd better relax for a while. It's still early—"

"Help me up," he interrupted her.

"Clint—"

"Okay, don't help me up," he said. He put his palms flat on the bed and pushed himself to a seated position. From there he swung his legs off the bed to the floor, but for a moment he couldn't seem to feel it.

"Shit," he hissed under his breath. He banged his feet on the floor to make sure it was there, and then started to get up. Halfway there he began to fall back, which is when Amy grabbed him by the arm and held him up.

"Thanks."

"If you insist on getting up I might as well help you," she said. "Where do you want to go?"

"Water basin," he said. She walked him over to it, poured him some water from the pitcher, then stood back with her arms folded across her chest while he vigorously washed his face.

Taking the towel she handed him he said into it, "How did I get here?" Then he took it away from his face and said, "How did *you* get here?"

"Same way you did," she said. "Your friend."

"What friend?"

"He said his name was Colorado Charlie."

"Charlie Utter."

"That's right. He said he found you wandering the street in the worst part of town. Apparently you'd been hopping from one saloon to the other. He found you before someone could take advantage of your condition."

"My condition," he said. He dropped his hands to his side, which made him think of his gun.

"Where's my gun?" he asked.

"Over by the window, hanging on a chair. He brought you back to your room, and then he came to get me."

"Why you?"

"He said he knew we'd become friends," she said. "We are friends, aren't we?"

"Sure—as long as I don't get your Uncle Jeff mad at me."

"Don't worry about Uncle Jeff," she said, touching his arm. "I can handle him."

He finished drying his hands and put the towel down.

"Maybe you should get to the office now, Amy," he suggested. "I'll be all right."

"Are you sure?" she asked. "Or are you just worried about my reputation?"

"It just might not look right—"

"You're a sweet man," she said, touching his cheek. "I'll go, but I'll see you later, okay?"

"All right," he agreed. "After court's adjourned."

"I'll be there," she said, "covering it for the paper. I'll see you there."

"Okay."

She walked to the door, then turned and said, "Don't be too hard on yourself, Clint. You must have had a reason, last night."

"No more than usual," he said. "No more than usual."

TWENTY

Clint got to the courthouse early enough to get a seat up front, where he could see every face. When Marshal Hanks got there, he came over and sat next to him.

"You okay?"

"I'm fine."

"I heard you had a bad time last night." A man entered the courtroom then and Hanks said, "Would you like to meet Colonel May?"

"The prosecutor?"

Hanks nodded. "He got special permission to prosecute the case. I think he takes it pretty personal that McCall got off the first time."

"I would, too," Clint said.

"Come on," Hanks said, standing up. It was easier for him than Clint, but the Gunsmith got to his feet and followed the lawman to the prosecutor's table.

"Colonel May?" Hanks said.

May turned around and said, "Marshal."

He was not a tall man, and his girth made him appear even shorter than he was. He had a strong face, though, and a determined look.

Clint instinctively felt that the man was a competent prosecutor.

"This is Clint Adams," Hanks said. "He's an ex-lawman, and he was a friend of Hickok's."

"I'm aware of Mr. Adams's reputation," the prosecutor said.

"Which one?" Clint couldn't help asking.

May looked at him and, extending his hand, said, "As a damned fine lawman."

"Thank you, Colonel," Clint said, feeling that the prosecutor was being sincere. "I'm sure you were pretty upset when McCall got off the first time."

"That trial was a farce!" the man replied, vehemently. "This time he won't escape justice, I can assure you of that. I will do my very best."

"I'm sure you will," Clint said. "Good luck."

"Thank you, Mr. Adams."

Clint went back to his seat and the courtroom was starting to fill up now.

"Is this seat taken?" a female voice asked from the aisle.

He removed his hat from the seat next to him and said, "No, it's not taken."

When the woman moved by him to take the seat there was something about her scent that was familiar. As she sat he looked at her, and she turned and smiled at him.

It was Billie, the saloon girl.

"Hi," she said.

"Good morning, Billie."

"For me, maybe," she observed, "but you look like you had a hard night."

Working where she did, she'd seen enough men looking the way he did the morning after to know.

"You look very . . . nice this morning," he said.

"You mean very proper, don't you?" she asked. The dress she was wearing this morning was far less revealing than anything she would wear at the saloon. As a matter of fact, the high-necked dress revealed nothing at all, although it couldn't conceal the fact that she was a very full-figured young woman.

"What are you doing here?" he asked.

"I'm interested in seeing what happens," she said. "After all, this could be a very famous day in history."

"I suppose that's true," Clint agreed.

He was looking around the courtroom now for familiar faces, and he saw a few. In the back of the room he could see Colorado Charlie, who nodded to him and sat in the back row. From Deadwood he saw Harry Young and Captain Massey, who were no doubt there to testify as eyewitnesses to the incident.

He looked around for Charlie Rich, the man who had refused to give up his seat for Hickok, but the gunman was nowhere to be seen.

And then across the other side of the room he spotted Amy Walker, who was staring at him—and, he realized, at Billie—with daggers in her eyes.

He smiled, and she nodded coldly and applied her attention to her notebook.

"Did I get you in trouble?" Billie asked.

"What?" he said. He saw her looking past him at Amy and then said, "No, of course not."

Before she could reply, the judge entered the court, and the announcement was made that court was in session.

The case against Jack McCall was underway.

TWENTY-ONE

The morning was taken up with opening statements. McCall's defense attorney was one Andrew Tyler, a young man who seemed entranced by the sound of his own voice. After he and Colonel May finished with their lengthy opening remarks, there was nothing left for the judge to do but recess for lunch.

"This is going to take longer than I thought," Clint said aloud.

Not only the young Tyler but May as well seemed intent on making some kind of a show out of this. May was almost passionate in his remarks to the jury, painting Hickok as a beloved legend of the West who was shot down in his prime by a coward. Well, at least he had part of that right. McCall was certainly a coward, but Clint didn't know exactly how beloved Hickok was, and he certainly hadn't been in his prime.

Judging from the condition of his eyes in Abilene

when Clint had served as his deputy, his eyesight had
to have been pretty deteriorated by the time that day
in Deadwood rolled around.

"You going to have lunch?" Billie asked him,
breaking into his thoughts.

"I'm not hungry," Clint said, which was true
enough. The mere thought of food made his stomach
lurch. His real reason, however, was that he wanted
to talk to Colorado Charlie and to Massey and Young
about the whereabouts of Charlie Rich.

As for Charlie Utter, Clint wanted to know if he'd
seen either Varnes or Brady since the first time.

"Then I'll see you back here after lunch," Billie
said. "Save me a seat, huh?"

"Sure."

Having sat in front of the room, Clint filed out at
the end of the group and once outside collared Colorado Charlie.

"How you feeling?" Charlie asked.

"Terrible," Clint replied, "and it's got nothing to
do with my head threatening to fall off."

Standing there with Charlie, Clint felt overwhelming embarrassment in front of this man, whose drinking he had been limiting the entire time they were
traveling together. He was embarrassed because it had
finally been he who had slid back into the bottle.

"I don't know what you're feeling so bad about,"
Charlie said. "How do you think I found you last
night?"

"What do you mean?"

"I bumped into you, Clint," he said. "I was coming
out of the saloon you were going into."

Clint eyed Charlie critically, wondering if the man
were telling him the truth or just trying to save him
any more embarrassment. True, Colorado Charlie's

eyes were bloodshot, but they had been that way since he'd met the man. He decided to accept Charlie's words at face value and not question whether they were true or not.

"All right, Charlie," he said, "as long as we're both back on the right path."

"Did you understand all of that talk inside?" Charlie asked, looking confused.

"Some of it, yeah," Clint replied, "but I think this trial is going to take a lot longer than I thought."

"It was just a lot of talk, nobody even asked anybody a question. I didn't even hear Bill's name mentioned but once," Charlie Utter said.

"Don't worry, Charlie. As long as McCall is found guilty, they can talk all they want. I've got something else I want to talk to you about."

"What?"

"Varnes and Brady. Have you seen them again?"

"Sure I did."

"Did they see you?"

"Couldn't help but see me," Charlie said. "They was both in court, Clint, sitting in the back row across from me."

"Did they say anything to you?"

"Didn't even look at me, but they saw me, all right. Why are you interested in them?"

"Somebody took a few shots at me yesterday."

"And you think it was Varnes and Brady?"

"Not necessarily," Clint said. "I mean, why would they shoot at me? How would they know who I was?"

"Them two wouldn't need no good reason to back-shoot somebody," Charlie assured him.

"But they got McCall to do it to Hickok."

"So maybe they got somebody else to shoot at you."

"Do you know of any gunmen who are in town?" Clint asked.

"You mean, besides you?"

Clint winced, but said, "Yeah, Charlie, besides me."

Charlie thought a moment, then said, "I ain't seen anybody I know."

"Neither have I," Clint said. "So let's find out if there's anybody in town we don't know."

TWENTY-TWO

Judging from the way the morning session went, Clint realized that there was no danger of the case being decided in one day, so he figured that he could miss the afternoon session.

"Clint," a voice called out to him outside the courtroom as the trial proceeded within. He turned and found Marshal Hanks bearing down on him.

"You being so interested in the trial, I'm surprised you're not inside."

"I'm interested in the outcome, Marshal," Clint said, "not all of the bull that's going to be flying."

"I feel the same way," Hanks said. "Between May and that young Tyler, this trial could go on forever."

"I hope not." Clint made a quick decision and told Hanks what happened the day before.

"You didn't get a look at him?" Hanks asked.

"Not a sign."

"It's not unusual for you to be shot at, is it, Clint?"

"No," Clint said, knowing what he was getting at.

"Somebody sees you in the street, recognizes you from somewhere . . . and decides to make a name for themselves."

"It's happened before," Clint agreed, "and it will happen again."

"Where would I look first, Clint?"

Which was precisely the reason Clint's first instinct was not to report the incident to Hanks.

"I just thought I'd let you know, Marshal," Clint said, "just in case somebody ends up dead in your town."

"I hope it doesn't come to that."

"So do I." Clint looked at the marshal, who was matching him stride for stride, and said, "Where are you off to now? Going back to the trial later?"

"I've got some business to take care of in my office."

"One of your deputies is with McCall?"

"Two of my deputies are in the courtroom, just in case, and yes, I'll be going back later. What about you?"

"Do you know of any gunmen who have come to town recently?"

"You mean besides—"

"Yeah, besides me," Clint said.

"None that I know of. Wouldn't another gunman face you rather than shoot you in the back?"

"Not if he didn't want to commit suicide," Clint said before he could stop himself.

Hanks digested that with raised eyebrows and then said, "Here's my office. Let me know if you find out anything. I'll help in any way I can. I don't want anyone dying in my town if I can help it."

"If I find out anything, Marshal, you'll be the first to know."

"I hope so, Clint," Hanks said. "I meant what I said. I don't want anyone getting shot down in my town."

"I couldn't agree more, Marshal."

Hanks crossed the street and entered his office, catching his deputy with his feet on the lawman's desk.

"Come to the window, Clem," he directed the younger man.

"Yes, sir."

"See that man?" Hanks asked, pointing.

"Yes, sir."

"I want you to be his shadow for as long as he's in Yankton."

"Uh, yeah?" the deputy said, looking confused.

"I want you to follow him, Clem, until he leaves town."

"And then what?"

Hanks was tempted to tell him to go right on following him out of town, but instead he said, "And then I'll give you new orders."

"Who is he?"

"He's a man with a target on his back," the lawman said. "Make sure nobody takes a shot at it."

"Right, Marshal."

When the kid deputy left, Hanks went over and sat behind his desk and took out a batch of new wanted posters. He looked at the top one, then put it down and sat back in his seat.

The lawman knew that Clint Adams was not the Gunsmith by choice, but he *was* the Gunsmith, and there was nothing he could do about it. Men like that responded only one way when they were getting shot at, so Hanks felt damned sure that today, tomorrow, or sometime between now and the end of the McCall trial, there was going to be a shooting and at least one dead body in Yankton.

He sincerely hoped that it wouldn't be Clint Adams.

TWENTY-THREE

Even though Clint and Charlie had split the town in half, Yankton was a big town, and Adams knew they couldn't hope to cover every foot of it. They were checking hotels and boardinghouses and Clint had dug into his waning poke and given Charlie enough so that he could grease a desk clerk's palm or two for a look at his register, which was what he was doing as well.

Later they met at Yankton House for a beer and compared notes.

"Nothing," Charlie said.

"Me, too," Clint echoed. "So as far as we know, there's no gunman registered in this town under his own name."

"Wouldn't take much money to make a back-shooter out of a saloon swamper," Charlie observed.

"Yeah," Clint agreed. "It happened before, right?"

Jack McCall, among other things, had been a saloon swamper in Deadwood, before he killed Bill Hickok.

"Something happened, though," Clint said.

"What?"

"I picked up a friend."

"Anybody I know?"

"I don't even know him," Clint replied. "The marshal has one of his deputies following me around."

"What did you do?"

"It's not what *I* did. I told the marshal I'd been shot at, and I guess he's trying to protect me."

"That the deputy?" Charlie asked, indicating the kid standing at the bar. They were seated at a corner table, with Clint in his usual chair.

"That's him."

"Imagine that."

"What?"

"The marshal giving a kid the job of keeping the Gunsmith alive," Charlie said, chuckling and shaking his head.

"Don't call me that to my face, Charlie," Clint said coldly.

"That's your name," Charlie said. "Bill always liked being called Wild Bill."

"That was Bill, this is me. I don't like being called . . . that name. I never have, and I never will."

"But it's who you are, Clint."

"That may be, Colorado Charlie, but don't call me by that name. Okay?"

Charlie Utter stared at Clint a moment, to see how serious he was, and when he saw the look in his eyes he said, "Anything you say, Clint."

They each picked up their beer and sipped during the awkward silence that followed.

"What do we do now?" Charlie asked, breaking the silence first.

"I suppose we might as well go over and see how the big trial is going. While we're there, I'll corner either Massey or Young, and you can point out Varnes and Brady to me."

"Why do you want Massey and Young?" Charlie asked. "Didn't you talk to them in Deadwood?"

"Yeah, but I also talked to Charlie Rich in Deadwood, and he lied to me. I'd like to know if either one of them knows where Rich is."

"Are you gonna go after Rich?"

"I'd like to know why he lied."

"Maybe *he* set Bill up," Utter said, as if he'd had a sudden inspiration.

"And maybe he was just afraid," Clint suggested. "I don't know. Maybe it doesn't even mean anything. Who knows?"

Clint picked up his beer mug, which was still half full, looked at it, and then put it down again.

"Look, why don't you go over to the courthouse and locate those two. Be ready to point them out to me when I get there."

"What are you gonna to do?"

"I'm just going to sit here a few minutes more and stare at that beer. I want to think."

Charlie gave Clint a look that said maybe he thought he was going to order a bottle of whiskey when Colorado left.

"I'll be all right, Charlie," Clint said, reading the other man's mind. "I swear, I'll be right along."

"Okay," Charlie said, standing up. "I'll see you later."

"In a few minutes."

When Charlie left Clint did just what he said he

was going to do. He stared at that half a mug of beer, wondering what he was really doing in Yankton.

He passed one hand over his face, but everything looked the same. Since he'd "retired" as a lawman, he'd been through quite a few changes, attitude changes, but never one this drastic. Lots of people lost friends, didn't they? Why did he and Bill have to be so special? Why did he have to be so special? If it had happened the other way around, would Bill be doing what he was doing? He doubted it very strongly.

What about when this was all over, one way or another? What kind of a change would he go through then? Where was the real Clint Adams, and would he ever be seen or heard from again?

When he finally stood up and left the saloon, he didn't really know who he was anymore, but whoever he was, he had to finish what he'd started.

At least that part of him stayed the same.

TWENTY-FOUR

When he reached the courthouse he was surprised to see that it was emptying out. He stood back and watched as the column of people became longer and longer, until at the very end he saw Colonel May.

Charlie came up next to him and said, "It was breaking up just as I was walking in."

"Why so early?" Clint asked. "It's only three."

"I'm not sure I understand, but it looks like that young lawyer said something real bad that the judge didn't like, and he's gonna have to spend the night in jail. The judge said something about him being con-content?"

"In contempt?"

"That's it."

Apparently, the young Mr. Tyler had tried some sort of courtroom trickery which the judge had not

approved of, and in doing so probably prolonged the
trial by as much as a day.

"Did you see Varnes and Brady?"

"Yeah. They're right over there, by the steps to
the courthouse."

Clint looked over and saw two men, one short, one
tall and lanky, talking together.

"That's them."

He started to look through the milling crowd and
said, "Now where the hell are Massey and Young?"

"They're both staying at the hotel down the block
from yours," Charlie said. Clint looked at him and
Utter added, "I saw their names while I was checking
the register. I forgot to mention it to you before."

"That's okay," Clint assured him. "Maybe I'll just
go over there and wait for them to show up."

"What do you want me to do?"

"If you think you can keep an eye on Varnes and
Brady without getting into trouble, why don't you do
that. If they look like they're going to give you a hard
time, then leave them be."

Clint turned around to see if his friend the deputy
was still there, and when he spotted him he said to
himself, "Well, let's go, Mr. Deputy."

He walked away from the courthouse, but before
he took five steps a voice called out from behind him.

"Clint?"

He recognized the voice as Amy's and turned to
find her trotting after him. She was wearing pants and
a man's shirt again, and her right hand was holding
an old stetson on her head that also looked too big.
She looked like a little girl dressed in her daddy's
clothes.

"Hello, Amy."

When she reached him she stopped, looked around and said, "Where's your friend?"

"My friend? You mean Colorado Charlie?"

"You know who I mean," Amy said, and it wasn't until that moment that he did.

"Oh, you mean Billie."

"That saloon girl."

"Why would she be with me?"

"She was looking all over for you once the trial started up again," she explained.

"Really? And what were you looking for?"

She stiffened her chin and said, "I'm looking for a story, naturally."

"Naturally. You going back to the office?"

"Yeah. I've got to do a piece on the trial for the early edition."

"How many editions has that paper of yours got?"

She grinned sheepishly and said, "One."

"Come on," he said. "I'll walk you back."

On the way she asked, "Why weren't you in the courtroom this afternoon? I thought you were interested in the trial."

He told her what he'd told Marshal Hanks about being more interested in the outcome.

"How did it go?" he asked.

"Just a lot of talk about what kind of a man Bill Hickok was," she said. "Colonel May was building him up as a paragon of virtue by asking the right questions, and Mr. Tyler was bringing out all the bad things by asking the wrong questions."

"Well, there was a lot of bad about Bill," Clint said, "but he wasn't a bad man. Even if he was, he still didn't deserve to get shot in the back."

She stared up at him and then said, "That's what

really bothers you, isn't it? I mean, Wild Bill was your friend and all, but what bothers you most of all is the way he died."

Clint hesitated, then replied, "The way he died bothers me, yeah. There's no dignity in that. It's obscene to die like that. It's—" He stopped short because he felt that rage building up inside of him and wanted to head it off.

"Here's your office," he said, unnecessarily.

"Where are you going now?"

"To talk to some people," he answered.

"Will you be at the trial tomorrow?"

"I don't know," he said. "It depends on a few things."

"Then . . . will I see you again . . . soon?" she asked, with unaccustomed shyness.

Clint looked at the pretty young girl in a man's clothes and said, "Why don't we have dinner again tonight?"

"All right," she agreed, her face lit up by a happy smile.

"I'll pick you up at seven."

"I'll be ready," she promised. Impulsively she kissed him on the cheek and then scooted into her office.

TWENTY-FIVE

Clint reached the hotel where Massey and Young were staying and found out from the desk that they hadn't come in yet. He went out in front and sat in a chair, content to wait until they did show up.

About ten minutes later, when the two men mounted the boardwalk to enter the hotel, Clint stood up and they stopped at the sight of him.

"Adams," Young said.

"Hello, boy. You mind if we have a little talk?"

"What about?" Massey asked. He was still holding his injured arm stiffly.

"This and that," Clint said. "Does this hotel have a bar?"

"No."

Clint looked around and spotted a small saloon across the street from the hotel.

"Let's go over there and I'll buy you boys a drink."

"We were just gonna get cleaned up—" Young started to say, but Clint interrupted him.

"I won't keep you long."

"Well," Young said, exchanging glances with Massey. "Okay."

The three men walked across the street in silence, with Young and Massey displaying some degree of nervousness.

"Why are you fellas so nervous?"

The two looked at each other, and Massey answered, "I don't know about Harry, but look what happened to me last time I sat down in a saloon with a—" He stopped short, unsure of how Clint would react to what he was going to say.

"With a what?" Clint asked. "With a gunfighter?"

"With a man with a reputation," Massey said.

"Well, I guess you might have a point, then," Clint said. "What's your excuse, Harry?"

"Hell, that crazy McCall tried to shoot me too and would have if his gun hadn't misfired."

As they reached the saloon, Clint said, "We'll just have to keep an eye out for backshooters, then, won't we?"

Inside Clint ordered three beers and carried them to a corner table.

"What's this about, Adams?" Young asked.

"It's about the same old thing," Clint answered. "I want to know who the man was that wouldn't give Hickok his seat, the one against the wall. How about it, Harry? You were tending bar, you must have been watching the game. Who was sitting with their back to the wall?"

"I'll have to think—"

"Just close your eyes and picture it," Clint said, cutting him off.

Young closed his eyes, and then he opened them and said, "I remember! I remember that every time Rich called for a drink, he held his hand up to me and I could see his full face. He was sitting facing the bar, so that means he had his back to the wall."

"That's right," Massey said.

"Do either of you know where Charlie Rich is now?"

They looked at each other, and Massey shook his head while Young said, "No."

"Was he in Deadwood when you left?"

"No," Massey said. "He left town the day after I talked to you in my hotel."

"Now let me ask you this, and consider it carefully, because his life may depend on it. Do you think Rich was setting Hickok up by not giving him his seat?"

"You mean, deliberately setting him up?" Massey asked.

"That's what I mean."

"No," Massey said, shaking his head emphatically.

"Why not?"

"Because Rich is a gunman as well as a gambler," Massey said. "He wouldn't do it to Hickok because he wouldn't want it done to him. Besides, he was afraid of Hickok. If it had backfired and Hickok was still alive, he would have killed Rich, and Charlie knew it."

"He lied to me about sitting in Hickok's place. If he wasn't involved, why would he lie to me?"

"I'd say he was afraid of you too and afraid of what you'd do if you found out."

"Why do you think Rich refused to give up his seat?" Clint asked Massey.

Massey shrugged. "He accused Bill of being superstitious, but I think it was the other way around.

The game was already under way when Bill came in, and Rich was winning. He didn't want to take a chance on breaking his streak."

It all made sense to Clint, and he found himself believing that Charlie Rich had nothing to do with Hickok's death.

"You gonna go after Rich?" Young asked.

"What for?" Clint asked. "For being a superstitious poker player?"

TWENTY-SIX

For dinner that evening Amy took the Gunsmith to a restaurant she said a stranger would never find.

"It's not in a better part of Yankton," she told him, "but I feel safe with you."

"Who do you usually go with?" he asked.

"Oh, Uncle Jeff and Gramps. I've been there with one or two other people—"

"Anyone special?"

"No," she said, "no one special. Not yet."

The restaurant was on a small, side street at the north end of town. The street was dimly lit, but the restaurant itself gave off a bright glow. When they reached it Clint could see that there was a good crowd inside, and Amy assured him that most of the customers were townspeople.

"What's the name of this place?" he asked Amy as they stepped inside.

"It doesn't have a name," she said. "It doesn't need one. Most of the people who eat here are regulars, and they come for the food, not for the name."

When they were inside a waitress approached and greeted Amy with a smile, calling her by name.

"Hello, Barbara," Amy said. "Could we get a table in a corner, please?"

She seated them at a small table.

"Menus?" the waitress asked.

"Since you know this place so well, why don't you order for both of us," Clint suggested.

Amy seemed surprised by the suggestion but pleased, and she went ahead and ordered.

"How old are you?" Clint asked suddenly as the waitress went to get their order.

"Why do you ask that?"

"I don't know," he said. "The question just came to mind. Don't you want to answer it?"

"I don't mind," she said. "I'm twenty."

His surprise must have shown on his face because she laughed and said, "I know, I look younger. What was your guess?"

"Eighteen."

"It was close," she said, smiling.

She looked quite different than she had for her day in court. She was wearing a simple dress which showed her trim young figure off to good advantage. Her breasts were small, but obviously firm and well rounded.

"How's your grandfather?" he asked.

"Oh, Gramps is fine. He's getting the paper finished up tonight. He insisted that I go to dinner."

"I'm glad he did."

"So am I."

They had dinner and chatted throughout, but Clint had a feeling that they both knew what they wanted that night. He wondered who would be the first to bring it up.

Over coffee, he received a surprise, because Amy leaned over the table, took his hand and said, "Clint, I want to go back to your hotel with you tonight." He was speechless for a moment and she asked, "Are you shocked?"

"I think so," he said. "Yes."

"So am I," she confessed. "I didn't think I would have the courage to say it, but now that I have, what do you say?"

"I want you to come back with me, Amy," he said. "There's no question of that, but what about—"

"What about my reputation?" she asked.

"Yes."

"I'm not worried about that, so I don't think you should be, either. Let's just finish our coffee and go to your hotel."

"Amy," he said, "there is something you should know."

"Some deep, dark secret?" she asked.

"No, there's nothing secret about it," he said. "Men like me, we're not very lucky to be around."

"That's funny," she said. "I feel very lucky being around you."

"I'm serious—"

"So am I, Clint," she said. She took both of his hands and he squeezed hers as she said, "You're not going to be able to talk me out of it, so you might as well stop trying. You'll make me feel unwanted."

Well, he certainly didn't want to do that, because she was anything but unwanted.

"All right," he said, "but the hell with the coffee. Let's go."

TWENTY-SEVEN

"I'm not a virgin," she said up in his room.

"You're not?" he said, slipping the dress over her head. She put her hands straight up in the air to help him and then stepped back and began to remove her underclothes.

"No," she added, "but I'm not very experienced, either."

"That's all right," he assured her, removing his shirt.

"I hope you're not disappointed," she said. She was naked by then, and he was anything but disappointed.

Her small, round breasts were tipped by dark brown nipples, while the hair between her legs seemed very fine, and a shade lighter than the hair on her head. Her brown eyes were very wide as she watched him undress, and became wider still when his enlarged penis came into view.

"Oh my," she said.

"What?"

"I've never seen one . . . quite that big before."

He approached her and asked, "How many b— men have you been with?" he said, catching himself before he could say "boys."

"One," she said. "He was young, and his wasn't nearly as big as yours."

"Was it that boy in the office?" he asked, kissing her neck as he gathered her into his arms.

"O-o-oh"—as their flesh came into contact— "David? No, it wasn't . . . him. Ooh!" she said, as she reached down to encircle him with her hands.

"What?"

"It's very hard and hot," she said. "His wasn't as hard."

"I see," he said. He tipped her chin up and kissed her, nudging his tongue between her lips.

"I told you I was inexperienced," she said. "I've never been kissed like that. With your tongue, I mean. Can I do it?"

"Sure."

He kissed her again, and her tongue tentatively pushed its way into his mouth. He grabbed it between his teeth and chewed on it gently while cupping her firm buttocks in his hands. He pulled her very close and his penis was nudging her belly.

"That's nice," she said, when the kiss ended. "Can we lie down on the bed now?"

"Sure," he said. He picked her up, which surprised her, and she threw her arms around his neck and held tight. He took a few steps across the room and gently deposited her on the bed and then lay down beside her.

"What else did you do with this . . . boy?" he asked, teasing her nipples with his tongue.

"Oh . . . nothing very much," she said. "We just kissed—but not the way we just did it—and then he put it in me."

"So you're just barely not a virgin," he said.

"I guess so . . . oh, what are you doing?" she asked suddenly.

He had reached between her legs and started fondling her, which made her jump and catch her breath.

"Just touching you," he assured her, "like this." He found her clit and began to roll it between his fingertips.

"Oh, that's . . . that feels so nice."

"Yes," he agreed. "It does."

He kissed her neck and then each breast in turn while he continued to fondle her. When she was wet enough, he dipped a finger into her, and then two. She began to move her hips, riding up and down his two fingers, and he continued to bite and suck on her nipples.

At that point she couldn't talk anymore. She simply made slow, rhythmic noise, like "Uhn . . . Uhn . . . Uhn . . . Ohh . . ."

He took his hand away from her vagina and began to inspect her body with his mouth and his tongue. He kissed her belly, licked her navel, ran his mouth over her thighs and calves, and then back up to her inner thighs, which he licked and nipped until his nose was buried in her pubic hair.

She smelled so fresh and clean, and he began to run his tongue up and down the length of her slit. Her moans became cries and she began to writhe beneath him. He reached underneath her, palmed her buttocks and lifted her hips off the bed. Holding her up like that he drove his tongue deep into the wet, sweet depths of her, and began to flick it in and out and around. Removing his tongue from inside of her, he began to once again lick her up and down, but this time he allowed his tongue to come in contact with her clit, and she started and cried out each time it did.

She was different from Billie in that the saloon girl's moves were very practiced, while Amy's moves were natural. The saloon girl knew what she wanted to do next, while Amy had no idea what was coming next.

When he reached her clit with his tongue again, he began to encircle it, rolling the little nub around and around until he could feel her belly quivering and her nub growing harder and harder. Suddenly she was flopping around, driving her bush into his face, grasping the sides of the bed with her hands, and drumming her heels in midair.

"Oh God . . ." she moaned as the tremors began to fade, but he wasn't going to give her any time to recover.

He let her buttocks lie on the bed again, then moved up between her legs. He poked at her moist portal, allowing the head of his cock to slide in and out a couple of times, and then little by little he began to feed her more and more of himself, until suddenly he jammed it in to the hilt and she buried her face in the pillow to muffle her scream.

"It's so big," she gasped. "It's filling me up. . . . It feels like it's here," she said, touching herself between her breasts.

"Is it uncomfortable?" he asked.

"Oh, no," she declared. "It's wonderful. I wish you could go even deeper."

"Here," he said, "put your legs around my waist . . . yes, like that. Now tighten them."

"Oh God, yes!" she said. "Yes, it feels like you're even deeper. God, I had no idea anything could feel so good."

"Hold on, now," he said, and he began moving in and out of her, slowly at first, but increasing his pace until she was panting, trying to keep pace with him.

"Oh . . . oh . . . oh . . ." she moaned, and he lowered his mouth onto hers so that she was moaning into his mouth.

He began to chew gently on her lips and her tongue, and then she began to do the same thing to him, and still he moved within her, in and out until she tightened her arms and legs around him even more and her hips began to bounce uncontrollably on the bed. At that point he released the control he had over himself and his seed began to spurt into her.

She pulled her mouth away from his and said, "God, what is that? It's so hot. Oh . . . it's so good. . . ."

And she kissed him again, sucking his tongue in frantically as he continued to fill her up. When his spasms decreased, and then stopped, she began to lick his lips playfully and he tried to catch her tongue between his teeth as she did so.

"Ouch," she said as he finally nipped her, and then she bit his bottom lip hard enough to make him say, "Ouch," too.

"This could get violent," he said, looking down at her.

"Good," she said, raking her nails over his back. "I'll leave my mark on you everywhere."

He laughed, and then when her face became very

serious, he said, "What's the matter?"

"I know I shouldn't ask this, because I'm going to hate the answer."

"Well," he said, "go ahead."

"Did you sleep with that—that saloon girl? No, wait," she went on quickly, "don't answer me. I know you did. How did I compare to her?"

As he opened his mouth to answer she said, "No, don't answer that, either. I don't want to know."

She turned onto her side, so that she wasn't looking at him, and he said, "Well, I'm going to answer you."

She squeezed her eyes shut and said, "Go ahead."

"There's no comparison," he told her.

She kept her eyes closed, and when she realized that he wasn't going to say anything further she opened them and turned to look at him.

"What does that mean?"

"It means that she can't compare to you."

"But I'm sure she's much more experienced. I'm sure she even did things to you that I . . . I don't know how to do."

"Maybe, but your reactions are so pure and so natural. She knows exactly how to react to what I do, and exactly what she wants to do next. There's much more mystery with you," he said, and then added, "And you taste much better."

"Really?" she said, looking pleased. "You mean . . . down there?"

"I mean everywhere," he said. He kissed her and ran his tongue over her lips.

"I didn't even know that men did the things with their mouths you did . . . down there."

"Oh, yes," he said. His penis was growing soft in her now, although it was still semi-erect at the moment. "And there are things that women do to men . . . *down there* too," he said, mimicking her tone.

She stared at him, to see if he was kidding, then narrowed her eyes and said, "Will you teach me?"

"Of course."

"Now," she said.

"Now?"

"We have all night," she said. "Or can't you— you're still big inside of me. Can you still—"

"With help from you, yes," he said.

"Then show me," she said. "Show me how to help you."

He withdrew from her and lay on his back next to her.

"Are you sure?" he asked.

"Yes, oh, yes," she said. "I'm very sure. I want to do everything with you, Clint. Everything that a man and woman should do together."

"Well, it's not really that they should," he tried to explain. "Some men and women don't like to do—"

"I will," she assured him. "I'll love it, only just show me, please?"

As if to influence his response, she grasped his semi-erect penis in her hand and began to stroke it. Surprised, she looked at the part of him she was holding and said, "It's growing, already."

"You see?" he said. "Some things just come naturally."

With her eyes shining she said. "Can I . . . use my mouth?"

"Of course."

She slithered down and examined his erect penis closely. She marveled at how she could take it in both hands, one fist on top of the other, and there was still more of it.

"That boy I told you about?" she said.

"Yes?"

"He wouldn't have filled both of my fists."

"Size doesn't mean a lot," he said. "It's how you use what you've got."

She stared up at him now, her eyes still shining mischievously, and slowly extended her tongue until it touched the head of his penis. Watching what she was doing now, she did that again, licking it slowly until it glistened with her saliva.

"I wonder how much I can take into my mouth," she said, half to herself. He did not answer, because he knew she wasn't talking to him. She was in a world of her own, now, learning new things, new sensations.

She slipped her lips over the head of his cock and enjoyed the way it felt in her mouth.

"Mmmm," she moaned as she sucked on it. Brazenly, she lowered her lips even further, taking part of the shaft into her mouth. It tasted bitter to her but not unpleasant, and it never dawned on her that she was tasting both of them.

To take more into her mouth now she had to remove one hand, keeping a tight hold on the base of the shaft with the other hand.

She began to suck harder and then moved her lips up and down the length of him. She knew she was making him feel good because he was moving his hips in time with her bobbing head, and she knew instinctively that she was doing the right thing to please him.

He was swelling even more in her mouth and suddenly she became afraid that if he came, she would choke. She allowed him to pop free and his penis suddenly felt cold.

"What happens if you—I mean, will I choke? Should I . . . swallow it?"

"Some women do," he said. "It depends on whether

or not they like the taste."

"How can I . . . taste it first?"

"Squeeze the head a bit." She did and he said, "There, see that drop? Lick it, see how you like it."

She licked the little white bead on the tip of his penis and tasted it experimentally.

"Well?" he asked. He had his hands behind his head and he enjoyed having this incredibly pretty, fresh-faced young girl peer up at him from between his legs. He felt more relaxed at that moment than he had in months.

"I'll try it again," she said. She squeezed him and when another drop appeared her tongue snaked out and captured it.

"Well?" he said again.

She grinned up at him and then opened her lovely mouth and took him in again. She began to suck, bobbing her head up and down faster and faster, and moving her fist up and down the base of his shaft. In no time she could feel him swelling up again, and she felt the tension in his thighs . . . and suddenly he was filling her mouth. She panicked a bit at first, but once she started to swallow she realized that she would be able to take it all. In fact, when he stopped spurting, she sucked on him until she was sure he was dry, and then she allowed him to pop free from her mouth.

"Jesus . . ." he said to her, and she smiled and crawled up to lie on top of him.

"It was wonderful," she said. "It tasted bitter, but it was very good."

"I'm glad you enjoyed it."

"Oh, I did," she assured him. She kissed him, gently at first, and then both their mouths opened at the same time and they were almost trying to devour each other.

"Clint," she whispered against his mouth.

"Mmm?"

"Can you . . . I mean, can you still—"

"You mean, again?" he asked.

"Can you?" she asked, eagerly.

"Are you trying to kill me, girl?"

"Oh, no," she said sincerely. "Never, never, never. Mmm," she moaned, kissing him again. Her eagerness and sincerity were not only overwhelming to him, but to his surprise he found them exciting. He felt that column of flesh between his legs beginning to stir again, and so did she.

"Oh, Clint," she cried. "You can!"

He grinned at her and said, "Damned if I can't."

TWENTY-EIGHT

They came into his room in the middle of the night, and as he went for his gun, Amy got in the way.

"Wha—" she said, sitting up, and as she sat up she came between him and the gun, which had been hanging on the bedpost. The Colt New Line and his Springfield rifle were too far away from the bed for him to reach them in time, and before he could even think about it, they were on him and dragging him from the bed.

"What are you—?" he heard Amy begin, but there was the sound of a slap, and her voice was cut off.

"Damn," he said.

They had dragged him from the bed so that his head and back had struck the floor hard. Each man had one of his ankles and he began trying to kick himself free.

It was too dark for him to see who they were, and

neither of them had spoken a word so far.

As he started to reach forward to try and release his ankles, he felt someone's boot strike the side of his face. The force of it drove him back down, and once again the back of his head struck the floor hard, causing him to see stars.

That's when he realized he was in for a beating.

Both of his assailants appeared to be very strong, and they remained silent as they took turns kicking him in the ribs on alternate sides. As a result of one kick he jerked so violently that his left ankle came free from the man's grasp. As the man reached for the ankle Clint kicked out hard and caught him partially on the chin and partially in the throat. The attacker staggered back, choking, and the sounds he was making were encouraging to the Gunsmith. Trying to ignore the pain in his ribs, he shifted over onto his right side, and kicked out with his left foot at the other man, catching him in the chest. The grip on his right ankle lessened, and he was able to pull free.

His eyes were accustomed to the darkness by now, and he could make out the shapes of the two men. They both appeared to be large, powerfully built men, and since he'd already felt their strength, his only thought was to get to one of his guns.

One man was still gagging, trying to get his breath, and as the other man lunged at Clint he tried to vault over the bed; only one foot caught on Amy, and he went sprawling.

Both men were on him quickly, one of whom was still breathing raggedly. As they went to grab him he threw one elbow back, hoping to catch the same man in the throat again. Instead, he felt his elbow strike the man's nose and the man howled in pain.

"Damn!" the second man shouted, and Clint felt a

powerful fist strike the side of his head, sending him sprawling. As he landed he knocked something over and then realized that it was his rifle.

His hands groped in the darkness for the weapon as one man advanced on him. As the man's shape loomed over him he felt his hand close around the barrel of the gun, and he swung it in an upward arc, catching the man a glancing blow on the face. As the attacker staggered back, Clint pointed the rifle at the ceiling and fired a shot.

"Shit, he reached his gun," a voice said, sounding hoarse and raw.

"L-let's get out of here," the other man said, sounding as if he had something in his mouth.

Clint was still only half aware of what was going on, but he realized that the two men had fled from the room, leaving the door open behind them.

He stayed on the floor, breathing deeply and trying to regain his senses. His ribs hurt like hell as he staggered to his feet and turned to look at the bed.

Amy was lying on her back, with one leg bent, which explained why he had tripped over her as he attempted to vault over the bed. As he approached her he could see that she was breathing normally and that there was a livid bruise on her right cheekbone.

"Amy," he said. He staggered as he reached the bed and put out his hands to steady himself. He took a few more moments to steady himself, then went to the water basin and dampened a towel. Using the damp towel to mop her brow and face, he started bringing her around.

"Amy," he said again, continuing to mop her brow.

"Uh, Clint?" Her eyes fluttered open and immediately she became frightened. "Clint!"

"It's all right," he said. "They're gone."

"Oh, are you all right?" she asked anxiously.

"Yes."

He stood up and she said, "Where are you going?"

"I'm going to light the lamp, and close the door," he said. "Don't worry."

When he had done so, he turned and looked at her in the light.

"Oh, Clint," she said.

"What?"

"You look awful."

He was bent over slightly, and now he wrapped his hands around his ribs and said, "I feel awful."

She got up out of bed quickly and went to him to support him and bring him to the bed.

"Is it your stomach?"

"Ribs."

When she moved his hands she could see the mottled bruises that were covering his ribs on both sides.

"Those animals," she said. "They kicked you."

"They sure did," he agreed.

She soaked a couple of towels in water and wrapped them around his ribs.

"Do you know who they were?" she asked.

"No," he said. "I couldn't see them in the dark."

"Did they say anything?"

"No."

"Why in God's name did they break in and beat you up, then?"

"I guess that's just something else I'm going to have to find out," he said.

"I'll go get Uncle Jeff," she offered.

"No," he said. "Stay here. It's too early to get him up."

"But . . . they might come back."

"They won't be back," he assured her. "The element of surprise is gone."

As she lay back in bed with him, he scolded himself severely; with him there should never have been any element of surprise.

He had allowed himself to relax too much, and because of that he did indeed have something else he was going to have to find out.

TWENTY-NINE

"Do you think it was the same man who shot at you, working with a friend, now?" Marshal Hanks asked in the morning.

After breakfast—which he had eaten alone, sending Amy back home—Clint had gone straight to Hanks's office to report the incident. The only thing he did not report was the fact that Amy had been with him.

"There's no way I can know that," Clint said, and then suddenly he remembered the deputy Hanks had put on his trail. "What happened to your deputy?"

Hanks made a face and said, "He stopped following when you went to dinner with Amy."

Clint thought he detected some tension in Hanks as he spoke of Amy Walker.

"I'll look into it," Hanks promised Clint. "I'll question the desk clerk at the hotel—"

"I already did that," Clint said. He had done so that morning, when he first came down from his room. "He says he didn't see anyone come into the hotel— but I'm pretty sure that for the right amount of money, he'd deny ever having seen me."

"You're probably right," Hanks said. "So, if you've done my job for me, why bother to come and report it to me?"

"You're the law, Marshal," Clint said. Somehow, he didn't feel that either of them wanted him to call the marshal by his first name just then.

"I'll ask around," Hanks said.

"Okay," Clint said. "Thanks."

"Are you going to be in court today?" the lawman asked.

"I don't know yet. Maybe."

"I'll see you then... maybe," Hanks said, and Clint nodded and left.

First shot at and then beaten. Those men had not come to his room to kill him, of that he felt sure. They were only supposed to beat him up. And they had been sent by someone else. He didn't know how he knew, or how he could be so sure, but he was. For the first few moments they were in that room, he was helpless, and if they had wanted to kill him, they could have.

How did that change the shooting incident? Was that actually an attempt on his life or some sort of warning? And what would be next?

On the boardwalk in front of the marshal's office he looked around. There were people on both sides of the street, but no one seemed to be paying any special attention.

He crossed the street and started looking for Colorado Charlie. He wanted to know if Charlie knew where Varnes and Brady were during the night, if they had left the hotel. For all he had seen of the two men in his room, they might have been Varnes and Brady, but as he recalled, Varnes was very tall and Brady was shorter. Both men in his room had appeared to be large, stocky, powerfully built men.

He went to the stable where he knew Charlie had slept and asked the man if he had come back to spend another night.

"Nope, didn't sleep here again, and didn't eat here. Does that mean you want your money back?" the man asked.

"No, keep it," Clint said, wondering where the hell Charlie had spent last night.

"Thanks, mister," the man said, but Clint was already walking away.

Walking through the alley where he'd been shot, he kept his hand on the butt of his gun and kept looking behind him, which annoyed him. He shook his head and hurried through the alley onto the main street.

Instead of making the rounds of hotels and rooming-houses again, Clint decided to go to the courthouse early and wait for Charlie. He also figured to watch the people as they arrived, specifically Varnes and Brady. He had done damage to at least one of his attackers last night, possibly breaking the nose of one. That kind of an injury would not be easy to hide. Perhaps one or both of the men would even be conspicuous by his absence.

He went to the courthouse, but positioned himself by a tree, and not directly in front of the building. He wanted to see without being seen.

Slowly the people began to filter in for the second day of the trial. He saw men with notepads, probably from out-of-town newspapers. He saw curious townspeople, who were coming just to watch the circus which he was sure Colonel May and young Mr. Tyler would make out of the trial. He remembered then that Tyler had spent the night in jail, probably conferring with his client. Did the young attorney really think that McCall was innocent, or was he just trying to make a name for himself through a celebrated case?

When Varnes and Brady finally showed up, neither man's face was marked at all. That let them out as the attackers of the previous night.

Who were they, then? And what kind of a threat did the Gunsmith pose that they would want him scared off?

THIRTY

Just before he was ready to go inside himself, Colorado Charlie Utter came along and started up the steps. Clint hurried after him to stop him before he entered.

"Charlie!"

Utter heard him and turned around as he reached the top of the steps.

"Oh, there you are," he said. "I thought you'd be inside."

Clint joined him on the top step and briefly told him what had happened during the night—leaving out the part concerning Amy Walker.

"You didn't see who they was?"

"Too dark," Clint said, shaking his head. "But I'm convinced that they weren't supposed to kill me."

"Why?"

"They had plenty of chances. When I grabbed my rifle they still could have drawn their guns and fired at me while I was on the floor, but they chose to run."

"Maybe they was afraid of you once you got your hands on a gun," Charlie suggested.

"Maybe, but I doubt it."

"Do you think they was Varnes and Brady?"

"The thought had crossed my mind, but at least one of them would have to have bruises or marks on their face, and Varnes and Brady don't."

"Who, then?"

"I don't know, Charlie," Clint said. "I don't know who or why, but I intend to find out."

"Well, I'll help you if I can," Charlie said.

Clint grinned and said, "I appreciate that, Charlie, I really do."

"Are you gonna go inside?"

"I don't think so," Clint said. "I think I'm just going to take a turn around town, maybe work up an appetite for lunch. I'll see you later."

"Right," Charlie said, and went into the courthouse.

Clint knew he was embarking on an impossible task, but while he was "working up an appetite" he was going to be on the lookout for a couple of powerfully built men with marks on their faces.

He started going in and out of the saloons, but it was a little too early for there to be many people drinking and after the third stop he realized how futile his plan was.

His fourth and last stop was in the saloon where he had met Billie, and he got a beer from the bartender and took a table in the corner. He was surprised to see the girl coming towards him a few minutes later, because he assumed she'd be in court watching the trial.

"You're not in court today, I see," she said, taking a seat across from him.

"Neither are you."

"What happened to you yesterday, after the lunch break?"

"I had some things to take care of."

"I'm sure you did," she said, in a tone that said more than her words did.

"What's wrong with you?" he asked.

"Nothing."

"Billie, I've known too many women to take 'nothing' as an answer to that question."

"Maybe that's the problem," she said.

"What is? You're not making sense."

"You know so many women," she said, "like that little news*boy!*"

"Oh," Clint said, getting the picture. She was talking about Amy Walker, but how did she know about Amy Walker? Or rather, how much did she know?

"I know a lot of people, Billie," he said, simply, "and I never account to one for knowing the other."

"Is that so?" she asked. "And I don't suppose you want to go upstairs for a little while, either?"

"Not particularly," he said, which he would have said even if he had felt like it.

"Of course not," she replied. "Not after last night."

He frowned and asked, "Just what do you know about last night, Billie?"

"I know a lot of things that go on in town," she said.

"Oh, you do?" he asked, with interest. "Tell me what went on last night?"

"As if you didn't—"

"Billie," he said, suddenly clamping his hand down on her arm, exerting enough pressure for her to know he was serious, "I want to know what *you* know about last night, and I want to know now!"

"Clint, that hurts—"

"Not yet it doesn't," he said. "But it could."

"You're serious," she said, looking into his eyes.

"Last night, two men broke into my room and tried to kick my ribs through my back," he told her. "I want to know what you know, and how you know it."

"Wait a minute," she said, "I think there's something wrong here—"

"Then explain it to me, and make it damned good."

"I don't know anything about you being beat up last night," she said. "All I know is that you had dinner with Amy Walker last night."

"That's all?"

"That's all."

"And what about that remark about my not wanting to go upstairs, especially after last night."

"Oh, that," she said. "That was just a guess. And a pretty lucky one, right?"

She stood up and he said, "Right."

"You're disappointed," she said. "I'm sorry I can't help you as far as those men are concerned."

"So am I."

"You know, you scared me a minute ago."

"Sorry."

"Let me know if you find those men, will you?"

"Why?"

"I'd like them to kick you a few times in the ribs for me," she said.

"No way," he said. "When I find those men, they'll

be sorry they ever kicked anyone, and they'll never kick anyone again."

She stared at him for a long moment, and said, "You know, you just scared me again," and walked away.

THIRTY-ONE

Clint started to rise from his chair but sat back down when the batwing doors opened and admitted two men. One man had a bruise on his face, and the other had a swollen, red nose, as well as a bruise. The man with the bruise alone had another very interesting feature: a black patch over the right eye, with a scar that ran through the eye and down to his mouth. Buckman and Hedge, the two men he had rescued Amos Walker from. And their faces were definitely marked.

Now there was one problem with this. He had already come to the conclusion that the two men were brawlers and they could have sustained their injuries in many different ways—including the possibility that they inflicted them on each other.

Still, the injuries were right, and both men were

153

big and powerful—and probably for sale. The only
definite way to find out was to ask them.

He stood and walked to the bar, where the two
men were receiving the beers they'd ordered.

"A beer," he said to the bartender. He stood with
enough space between them for three men, and watched
them. If they had heard his voice, they did not ac-
knowledge the fact. He figured they hadn't seen him
when they came in, either.

When the bartender brought him his drink, he asked,
"Have those men paid for theirs yet?"

"No."

"They're on me, then. You can let them know."

The bartender shrugged indifferently and said,
"Okay, friend."

He walked down to where Buckman and Hedge
were standing and informed them that they wouldn't
have to pay for their drinks. The two of them ex-
changed glances and then looked down the bar at
Clint. He was watching their eyes, and when they saw
him their eyes told him that he was right. They were
the men who had broken into his room the night before.

"Gentlemen," he said, holding his beer aloft.

Buckman made some kind of a move, but before
it could gain direction, Hedge stopped him.

"Hello, friend," the man with the patch said.
"Thanks for the drinks. I guess there's no hard feelings
about the other night."

"Not between you and me," Clint said. "Not about
the other night, anyway. How about last night,
though?" Clint added. "Now there are some very definite hard feelings about last night."

"What about last night?" Hedge said, touching a

thumbnail to his eye patch. "We didn't see you last night."

"No, and I didn't see you either," Clint said, "because it was so dark. You boys didn't even give me the courtesy of lighting a lamp before we had our chat."

"Friend, we don't know what you're talking about," Buckman said, "but if it's trouble you're looking for—"

Buckman stopped short, the result of a hard nudge from Hedge. Buckman was the big talker, the threatener, the pusher, but it was Hedge who made the decisions, and who was the deadlier of the two. He was the one Clint was most concerned with. In fact, if the two had been sent to beat him up, he was sure Hedge knew who hired them, but he wasn't sure Buckman did. Buckman would do it simply because Hedge said to.

Buckman moved away from the bar now, in direct defiance of Hedge. His pride was probably hurt, because he was the one who had been struck in the nose, he was the one who had first lost his grip and allowed Clint to get away.

"Mister," he said, "if you got something to say, you better go ahead and say it."

"I will," Clint said, "but I'll say it to Hedge. He's got the brain to understand it. You just stand there and look mean, maybe it'll scare me away."

Hedge laughed uproariously at that, which made it ever worse for Buckman to take.

"He got you there, Buck," the man with the patch told his partner.

"Let me kill him, Hedge," the other man pleaded.

"Shut up, Buckman," Hedge said. "You'd be dead

before your hand touched your gun."

The way that sounded, Clint had been right. Hedge had taken the job and knew who he was. Buckman didn't know.

"Hedge—"

"Buck, shut up."

"Stop tellin' me to shut up!" Buckman shouted, not taking his eyes off of Clint. He was tense, muscles bunched, and his right hand dangled near his gun, but Clint wasn't worried about his gun, because the man obviously was not a gunman.

"Hedge, if he doesn't ease up, he's going to end up dead," Clint told the scarred man.

"That's his business, Adams," Hedge said. He watched Buckman, but he was so incensed that he either didn't hear what Hedge had called Clint, or he didn't much care.

In which case, he was dumber than even Clint thought he was.

"All I want is a name, Hedge," Clint said, "and you both walk out of here."

"I can't do that," Hedge said, shaking his head slowly.

"I ain't walking out," Buckman insisted, obviously unaware of how that sounded.

"That's what I said, Buckman," Clint said, "unless I get a name from one of you."

"We should have killed you last night," Buckman said, seething.

"Buckman, you have got the biggest mouth...." Hedge said, trailing off. "Now we just about have to kill him."

"Or try," Clint said. "I wouldn't suggest it, Hedge."

"Believe me, it's not something I want to try and do," Hedges said, "but you'll go to the law now."

"Not if you give me a name."

Hedge seemed to be considering Clint's suggestion, but Buckman wanted to go for his gun, and he
decided that if he did, Hedge would back his play.

"Die, you—" he started to say, going for his gun.

Clint was leaning against the bar. He dropped his
hand to his gun almost leisurely, drew and fired before
Buckman touched his weapon—as Hedge had pre-
dicted.

The big man's eyes bulged as he stared at Clint,
and then the light in his eyes went out and he fell.
Clint swung his gun towards Hedge, but the scarred
man had his powerful hands in the air.

"Not me, Adams," he said. "I ain't crazy enough
to draw on the Gunsmith."

"He didn't know?" Clint asked, indicating the dead
man.

"He only knew what I told him," Hedge said, "and
all I told him was that we were hired to give you a
little beating." Hedge shrugged his thick shoulders
and said, "Nothing personal, friend."

"No, nothing personal," Clint said, holstering his
gun. "I want that name, Hedge."

"Sure, Adams, sure," Hedge said. "What's a name?
Can I put my hands down and drink my beer?"

"Do what you want, just so long as you give me
a name."

"A name," Hedge said, picking up his beer mug.
"Well, why not. The guy paid us already. Uh, you
wouldn't consider paying me for the information,
would you?" the man asked, narrowing his eyes
shrewdly.

"I've already paid you," Clint said. "You're alive."

"You wouldn't shoot me down," Hedge said.

"You're wearing a gun," Clint said. "When your

partner went for his, I could have assumed you'd back his play, and I could have killed you, too."

"But then you wouldn't get the name, would you?" Hedge asked, drinking deeply from his beer.

"I haven't gotten it yet—" Clint started to say, and then with surprising speed, Hedge's beer mug was flying towards him.

He could have drawn and killed the man then and there, but he wanted that name. He hesitated, and Hedge moved more quickly than he would have thought, closing a powerful hand over Clint's right wrist.

"Go ahead, Mr. Gunsmith, pull your gun now," Hedge said, grinning into Clint's face.

Clint tried, but he couldn't move his hand against the man's iron grip.

"Can't, huh?"

"No," Clint admitted. "I can't, but I still want that name."

Using his other hand, Hedge plucked the Gunsmith's gun from his holster and tossed it over the bar, where the bartender was standing and watching, as he had been the whole time.

"You stay where you are, bartender," Hedge advised the man. "Stay there and you stay healthy."

"I ain't goin' nowhere, mister," the man replied.

"The name, Hedge," Clint said again.

"You still asking for a name, friend?" Hedge asked. "Now that I've pulled your tooth? Ha!" With the exclamation, Hedge backhanded Clint across the face, sending him sprawling across the floor. He knocked over a spitoon at the foot of the bar, but avoided contact with the contents.

"Mister, you just killed the only friend I had," Hedge said. "He was dumb and bullheaded, but he was my friend, and you killed him, so now guess what I'm going to do to you?"

"You're going to give me the name I want, Hedge," Clint said from the floor, "or you'll end up just like your friend."

"You're crazy, man," Hedge said. "I'm gonna take you apart with my bare hands, because that's what I do best. We're gonna see how much of a legend you are without your gun."

Clint stood up and dusted off his pants, which got a rise from Hedge.

"You gonna stand up to me?"

"Well I'm not just going to let you run over me, Hedge," Clint told him. "Us legends have to uphold our names, you know."

Hedge smiled, and then laughed out loud.

"You know something?" he said. "It's too bad you killed my friend, because I like you." He turned to the bartender, dug into his pants and threw some money on the bar.

"What's that for?" the bartender asked, dubiously.

"Damages," Hedge said, and he charged Clint.

The Gunsmith sidestepped quickly, avoiding the lunge altogether, although he was again impressed by the big man's speed. Hedge went right on by him, ran into a table and splintered it.

He rose laughing and brushing woodsplints from his clothes and his sandy hair.

"You move good," he told Clint.

"Thanks."

"The man who took out my eye moved good," Hedge said, circling towards the bar. Clint circled with him, until Hedge's back was to the bar. "When I killed him, he still had my eye in his hand. He'd taken it out with a knife, and you can see what he did to my face," Hedge added, running his thumb along the scar. "I killed him anyway."

"I'm impressed."

"I think a man's got to have scars, if he's lived for a while. You got one there on your left cheek. How'd you get it?"

"Bullet."

"That figures."

He came towards Clint now, more deliberate, with his long arms widespread. Clint charged him, throwing a right from the floor which landed on the big man's left cheek. Hedge took it, then threw a punch of his own which made the air whistle. Clint moved his head but could not avoid the entire force of the punch. It drove him back into a chair, which splintered not from his weight, but from the force generated by the punch.

Hedge turned around and looked at the money he'd thrown on the bar, nodded, and started to advance on Clint again.

"I hope you got enough money for all of the damages," he told Clint. "I put my whole poke on the bar, there, but I don't think it's going to be enough."

"Oh, it'll be enough," Clint said from the floor. His face throbbed, and his ribs were reminding him of what he'd already gone through the night before.

"You think so?"

"I know so," Clint said, "because there aren't going to be any more damages."

As he rose to his feet, he reached inside his shirt and came out holding the Colt New Line and pointed it at Hedge.

"Shit," Hedge said. "I'm disappointed in you."

"I'm a little disappointed in myself," Clint said, "but what can I do? My ribs still hurt from last night."

Hedge had stopped about six or seven feet from Clint, and now he grinned and said, "You think that little gun's gonna stop me?"

"Hedge, this little gun will take out your other eye," Clint said, "and the slug will keep right on going through to your brain and then take off part of the back of your head."

Hedge made a face and said, "That sounds even more gruesome than this," indicating the scar on his face.

"And a lot more permanent."

Hedge dropped his hands to his side and relaxed his shoulders.

"Move," Clint told him, jerking the barrel of the gun to his right. Hedge, keeping a sharp eye on the gun, did as he was told, and Clint walked to the bar.

"My gun, please," he told the bartender.

The bartender retrieved his gun and handed it to him. He returned the New Line to his belt and pointed his gun at Hedge.

"The name, Hedge."

"The name, the name," Hedge repeated. "Take it and to hell with you and it."

"Well?" Clint prompted.

"Varnes," Hedge said finally. "The man's name is Johnny Varnes. I'd like to have a beer now, and then take care of my friend."

"Go ahead," Clint said, holstering his gun, "and forget about revenge, Hedge. Your friend got what he deserved."

"I know that," Hedge said, walking to the bar and staring at the bartender until the man gave him a beer. He drank deeply from the mug, then watched the Gunsmith's back as he walked out of the saloon, knowing that if he ever tried to draw and shoot the man in the back, he'd be dead in a second.

He looked down at his dead friend, whose head was turned towards him, with the mouth half-opened, as if he were going to speak.

"Shut up, Buckman!"

THIRTY-TWO

Clint went right to the courthouse, looking for Johnny Varnes, but when he got there he found that they had broken for lunch.

"Damn," he said, standing just inside the doorway of the empty courtroom. At least, he'd assumed it was empty. He hadn't seen the lone man sitting up front until he spoke.

"Do you have a problem?" Colonel May, the prosecutor asked.

Clint started, but when he spotted the man he walked down the aisle towards him.

"I was just looking for someone," Clint said. "How is your case going, Colonel?"

"It would be going much better—and faster—if young Mr. Tyler would stop trying to make a name for himself with long-winded preambles and theat-

163

rics," the man said. "But I think I can safely predict a conviction."

"That's good to hear."

May looked up at Clint curiously and asked, "Were you very good friends with Hickok?"

"He was the best friend I ever had."

"Would you like to get on the stand and say that?"

"How would that help?"

"It would let the jury know what an honorable, trustwor—"

"Hold on," Clint said, cutting the man off. "I didn't say any of that. I said we were friends."

"Yes, but—"

"Bill was my friend, but that didn't make him honorable or trustworthy or faithful or any of those things you said about him during the first day of the trial. The man wasn't perfect by any means, but then none of us are."

"I was only trying to make the jury see—"

"You were trying to make them see the man you wanted Hickok to be, or the man you thought he should have been, not the man that he was."

"I beg your pardon."

"McCall is guilty, May, but before he can be hung for his crime, you and his attorney may talk him to death."

"I'm doing the best I can do—"

"For whom?" Clint asked, cutting him short. "Certainly not for justice. The best justice is a quick justice. Do you know who told me that? Wild Bill Hickok. Which tells you what he would think of proceedings such as these."

"I don't think you're qualified to speak in the name of justice," May said, "no matter how many years you wore a badge."

"I took off my badge when the price of justice became too high, Colonel."

"I'm sorry you feel that way, Mr. Adams," May said. "I believe in due process—"

"It's a shame you don't believe in justice, Colonel," Clint said, and stormed out of the courthouse, looking for Johnny Varnes, for whom he had plans for his own kind of justice.

THIRTY-THREE

Instead of looking for Varnes, Clint went searching for Colorado Charlie Utter. He had offered to help, and Clint would let him do so, by finding Varnes for him.

He found Charlie in the Yankton House, which had pretty much become his drinking place—when he had the price of a drink.

"Charlie," Clint said, joining him at the bar.

"What happened to you?" Utter asked. "You got a brand new bruise on your face."

Clint touched the spot on his face where Hedge had hit him, and found it tender to the touch.

"Have you seen Varnes?"

"Only at the trial. Why?"

He explained what happened with Buckman and Hedge, and how Hedge had given him Varnes's name

as the man who sent them to his room the previous
night.

"Did you believe him?"

"Yes," Clint said. "Oddly enough, it never entered
my mind that he might be lying."

"So now you want Varnes and Brady."

"Nothing was said about Brady."

"You find one, you find the other," Charlie said.
"If Varnes paid to have you beat up, part of the money
came from Brady's poke, you can count on that."

"All right, one or both, then."

"You want me to see if they're at their hotel?"

"Yes, but don't let them see you. If they're there,
just come back and let me know."

"And if not?"

"Locate them for me."

"What are you gonna do?"

"I'm going to sit here and decide what I'll do with
them when I find them," he said. He recognized his
initial reaction as being excessive. He'd calmed himself since storming to the courthouse, and then out of
the courtroom after talking to May. And then he remembered seeing May talking to Varnes and Brady
in front of the courthouse the day before.

"What's their connection with May?"

Charlie looked surprised and said, "None that I
know of."

"When you pointed them out to me yesterday, they
were talking to him. You don't recall ever seeing them
together in Deadwood?"

Charlie thought a moment, then said, "No, I never
saw them together."

Clint frowned, and then said, "All right, go and
find them for me, and watch yourself."

"Right."

It was time now to go and see Marshal Jeff Hanks who, by now, might even have been looking for him. He'd killed a man after all, and Hanks was bound to be a little upset about that, no matter what the reason.

At Hanks's office he found the deputy who had been following him but not Hanks himself.

"Hello, Deputy," he greeted, shutting the door behind him.

The deputy jumped to his feet and seemed uncertain as to how to react. Obviously, he had heard about the incident in the saloon that morning.

"I'm looking for the marshal," Clint said.

"He's—uh—he's looking for you," the deputy stammered.

"Well, good. I'll just sit for a while and wait for him to get back, then," he said, pulling up a chair. "That is, if you don't mind, Deputy."

"Uh, no sir, I don't mind," the deputy replied nervously.

"Good." Clint sat and, for a few moments, he watched the young deputy fidgeting around from foot to foot.

"Aren't you the deputy who was tailing me?" he asked, suddenly.

"Uh, yes sir, I am."

"Why did you decide that I didn't need any more tailing that night when I went to dinner, son?"

The boy swallowed hard and said, "Well, uh, seeing how you was with Miss Amy, and seeing how Marshal Hanks is real close to Miss Amy, I didn't think he'd want me, uh, tagging after her—"

"What do you mean, about the marshal being real close to Miss Amy?"

"Uh, listen, mister, I gotta go and find the marshal," the deputy said, stumbling over his own feet in his haste to get to the door. "He's gonna want to know that you're here."

Sitting alone in the office brought back some old memories for the Gunsmith. He didn't relish running through them all again. He was about to get up and leave when the door opened and Hanks walked in.

"Marshal," Clint greeted.

Hanks scowled at Clint and walked over to sit behind his desk.

"Your deputy just went looking for you—"

"I been looking for you all morning," Hanks said, interrupting him.

"I figured you would," Clint said. "That's why I'm here."

"Damn it, Adams, I told you I didn't want no deaths in my town while you were here."

"I had no choice, Marshal. The man drew first—"

"I heard all about it," the lawman said.

"From who?"

"The bartender and Hedge."

"Well then, you know the whole story."

"Yes, I do," Hanks said, "and I'm only sorry I can't order you out of town because of what you did, but their stories were the same. You had no choice."

"So then what's the problem?"

"The problem is I have a dead man on my hands, and I don't like dead men."

"Did Hedge or the bartender tell you how the whole thing started?" I asked.

"The bartender said something about you hollering for a name the whole time," he said. "That's all he knew."

"What about Hedge?"

"He said that you drew last and fired in self defense, but he did not say what prompted the whole thing. He also said you could have killed him, but didn't. I guess we have to be grateful for that."

"Do you want to know what started the whole thing?"

"I suppose I should."

"Don't be so eager."

"And don't be so goddamned smart!" Hanks fired back. "I could still find some reason to order you out of town."

"But you'd need a lot of help to get me to go," Clint added.

Hanks glowered across his desk at Clint, then took a deep breath and let it out slowly.

"We're bumping heads," he said.

"That's right, we are," Clint agreed.

They stared at each other for a few moments, and then Hanks said, "All right, tell me about it."

He laid it out for Hanks, telling him how the marks on the faces of the two men had made him suspicious enough to approach them in the saloon.

"If I had been sure that Hedge wouldn't back Buckman's play," Clint added, "I might not have had to kill him, but I couldn't take that chance."

Hanks, pursing his lips and tapping a pencil against the top of his desk, finally said, "No, I guess you couldn't."

"Still want to run me out of town?"

Hanks made a face and said, "It may not have been your fault, Adams, but you attract that kind of thing. You can't help it."

"Like Hickok?"

"Yes, damn it, like Hickok." Hanks leaned forward and said, "Look, Clint, you're not even going to the courtroom. Why don't you leave town? You could read about the verdict in the newspaper—"

"I want to be here when the verdict comes in," Clint said, not allowing the lawman to finish. "I don't want to read about it in a newspaper."

Hanks, looking annoyed still, said, "All right, then, get the hell out of here, and try not to kill anyone else."

THIRTY-FOUR

Clint's temper was boiling, his stomach was churning, and he found that he wanted a drink. He also knew he wasn't going to have one, yet he had to go back to the saloon and meet Colorado Charlie.

When he reached the saloon he saw Charlie sitting at the table and walked directly to him, bypassing the bar.

"Where you been?" Charlie asked.

"Bumping heads with the marshal," Clint said, seating himself with his back to the wall.

"What?"

"Forget it. Where's Varnes?"

"I don't know."

"What do you mean, you don't know? Didn't you check his hotel?"

"I checked it, and he checked out."

"What about Brady?"

173

"I keep telling you, it's the same thing. Varnes, Brady, if one gets shot, the other one dies."

"So they're both gone. Just from the hotel, or from town, I wonder?" Clint said.

Charlie shrugged and drank his beer.

"Were their names brought up in court at all?"

"Not while I was there."

"What would have spooked them, then?" Clint said aloud, and he was actually asking himself the question. Had they heard about what had happened with Buckman and Hedge? Had they heard about it *from* Hedge? "They must know what happened this morning, but I don't think they would have left town, yet. Not while there's still a chance that McCall will mention their names. I want to find Varnes, Charlie. Keep looking."

"All right, but what do you plan to do when you find them?"

"I'm going to talk to them," Clint said. "I think I'm just going to talk to them."

Charlie gave him a look that said that he thought Clint was planning to do much more than that, but he shrugged and said, "I'll do my best to find them, if they're still in town. Where will you be for the rest of the day?"

Standing up, Clint said, "I guess I might as well go over to the courthouse and see how the trial is going."

"I never heard so much talk before," Charlie said as they walked out of the saloon. "Not even at the trial in Deadwood."

"Colonel May handled it different in Deadwood?" Clint asked.

"He made more sense there," Charlie said. "Here

he just seems to talk and talk and talk and not make any sense."

For the better part of a week Clint sat in on the court sessions, and he had to agree with his friend: May was just as publicity-hungry as his young opponent. Meanwhile Colorado Charlie prowled the streets of Yankton, looking for Johnny Varnes and Tim Brady. Neither he nor Marshal Hanks seemed to be having much luck finding them, but Clint had the feeling that of the two Charlie Utter was the one working the hardest at trying.

Clint's relationship with the lawman seemed to be getting worse and worse, until it reached the point where even a simple greeting from the Gunsmith brought a scowl from the marshal.

Clint continued to see Amy Walker; her innocent sensuality was a constantly renewed pleasure and made Clint's nights several times more interesting than his days.

Colonel May and young Tyler were still dragging the proceedings out, and as the week wore on, each man kept drawing his share of warnings from the judge for theatrics and threats of being held in contempt. Both men were already in contempt, as far as the Gunsmith was concerned. The trial was turning into a farce, which Clint felt was an insult to the memory of Bill Hickok.

By the second week there was still no sign of an end to the McCall trial. The judge and the people of the town were beginning to get very impatient, but none as impatient as Clint. He felt that everything hinged on the trial ending—and ending with a conviction. He wouldn't be able to put his life back in order until that happened—and maybe not even then.

On the seventh day of the trial, Clint met Charlie at the café as usual for breakfast. But something in the other man's face told him that this morning was going to be different. Charlie Utter had already ordered a pot of coffee; Clint poured himself a cup and took a swallow of the strong black brew.

"Charlie," he said. "What have you got?"

"Maybe something, maybe nothing," Charlie said. "I heard from a couple of drifters that there are two men up in Bragg who seem to be very interested in the outcome of the trial here."

"How far is Bragg?"

"Half a day's ride north," Charlie said. "Unless you push it, that is."

It didn't have to mean anything, but Clint felt his heart begin to race just the same.

"In that case," he told Charlie Utter, "let's finish up breakfast and push it."

THIRTY-FIVE

As much as they were pushing it to get to the town of Bragg, Clint was wishing he could push it even more, but that would have left Colorado Charlie behind. They had gotten him the best horse they possibly could, but the powerfully built spotted gray was still no match for Duke.

"What are we gonna do when we find them?" Charlie asked along the way.

"You can do whatever you want with Brady," Clint said. "Hedge told me that he was paid by Varnes, so Varnes and I are going to have a private talk."

"Why do you think he hired Hedge and his partern?"

"That's what our private talk is going to be about," Clint said. "The answer should be interesting."

"Are you going to kill him?"

Clint threw Charlie a sharp look, but the man had

simply asked a question, with nothing more than simple curiosity prompting it.

"I don't plan on killing him," Clint answered. "But then I can count on one hand the number of men I've planned on killing in my lifetime."

"And did you?"

"Yes."

Jesus, Clint thought, *I sound just like a young guntough trying to impress somebody.*

"Charlie, I've spent most of my life trying not to kill people," he explained. "Unfortunately, others have not always cooperated with me."

"Bill used to say you were the best man with a gun he ever saw," Charlie said, "but you didn't like using it. He wondered a lot what you would have been like if you liked using your gun."

"I've wondered the same thing about myself from time to time," the Gunsmith admitted.

They cut into the half day's ride by a few hours, and Charlie Utter's horse was lathered and winded. Duke, on the other hand, could have gone farther if necessary.

As they dismounted in front of the Bragg livery stable, Charlie shook his head admiringly at Duke and said, "That animal ain't human."

Clint smiled, patted Duke's neck and said, "He'll take that as a compliment, Charlie. Let's get them taken care of and then wash away some trail dust."

"Right."

They left the horses in the care of the liveryman, who was told to take special care of both of them. Clint wanted both animals ready if they were needed. After that they walked to the nearest saloon, had a beer and then went in search of Varnes and Brady.

They didn't have to search for long. There were

two hotels in town, and at the second one the desk clerk reacted to their descriptions of the two men. Money changed hands and the clerk gave them a room number on the second floor.

On the way up Clint said, "I'll go in first. Show your gun, Charlie, but don't fire it unless you absolutely have to. I want Varnes alive, if possible."

"You're the boss."

On the second floor they worked their way silently towards the room and stopped right outside. Charlie drew his gun, but Clint left his in his holster. He knew he could get it out fast enough if need be. Without speaking he conveyed to Charlie his intention to kick the door open and go in first. Charlie nodded, and waited.

Clint backed off, lifted his right leg and kicked out violently. His boot bottom came into contact with the door right above the doorknob. Wood splintered and the door swung inward, and Clint followed it in, with Charlie right behind.

There were two beds inside, and a man on each one. Both men sat up and stared, and then they both moved. Furthest from the window was Tim Brady, and he got off the bed and started towards his gun, which was on a chest by the wall. Varnes leaped off the other bed and grabbed his gun from the bedpost, but while Clint shouted—"Don't!"—Varnes kept right on going and threw himself through the window near his bed.

"Damn!" Clint shouted. "Charlie, keep Brady covered. I'm going after Varnes."

"Right."

Clint went through the window after Varnes, hoping he wouldn't have to kill the man to stop him. Directly outside the window was a porch, and Clint moved to the railing and spotted Varnes running down an alley, having obviously dropped down from the porch. He lifted himself over the railing, dropped down and started after him.

_ Varnes was wearing his pants and boots, but no shirt. He had strapped his gunbelt on while he was running, and was holding his gun in his right hand as he continued to run.

"Varnes!" Clint shouted. "Stop!"

Varnes showed no sign of stopping and Clint continued after him, his gun still holstered.

The alley opened onto a back street, and Clint slowed down only long enough to determine whether or not Varnes had stopped and was waiting for him to come out of the alley. As it turned out, he needn't have bothered. The only thing on Johnny Varnes's mind was getting away from the Gunsmith—alive!

Clint came out into the street and saw Varnes running towards the livery stable.

"Varnes!" he shouted again, but he knew it wouldn't do any good. He was going to have to run the man down and stop him, without killing him, and without getting himself killed.

He followed Varnes down the street and was surprised that the man never turned to fire at him. Why else would he have his gun in his hand unless he planned on using it?

Clint was gaining on Varnes, but the man still disappeared into the livery with Clint some yards behind him. If Varnes got on a horse, Clint's only way of stopping him might be with a bullet.

Instead of stopping and entering the livery with care, Clint threw himself through the door, landed on the ground and kept rolling, expecting to hear a shot.

Instead, he heard a man's voice from the back of the livery, cursing and babbling. He stood up and moved towards the back until he spotted Varnes. The man was trying to saddle a horse without letting go of his gun, and the obvious panic that he was in was not making it any easier.

"Varnes!" Clint said, and Varnes jumped, dropping the saddle and blanket.

"Adams!" he said. His voice quavered and the fear was plain in his eyes. As he backed away from the Gunsmith, the gun in his hand was all but forgotten.

"Settle down, Varnes," Clint said. "I just want to talk to you, that's all."

"Talk?" Varnes asked. "About what?"

"About a couple of men in Yankton that you hired to kick my ribs in," Clint said.

"I don't know w-what you're t-talking about," Varnes stammered.

"Sure you do," Clint said, keeping his eye on the man's gun. If Varnes made a move to use it, he wouldn't have any choice but to defend himself.

"I'm not interested in you, Varnes," Clint said. "Let's get that straight. I don't have any proof that you pushed Jack McCall into killing Hickok—"

"That's not true!"

"—but I do have proof that you hired Hedge and his partner to break my bones. What I want to know is why?"

"I didn't—"

"Varnes, if you think you're going to get out of here without answering me, then you had better use that gun in your hand."

Varnes looked down at the gun in his hand as if he had forgotten all about, and then he looked up at the Gunsmith. In a sudden, convulsive movement, he thrust the gun away from him, throwing it to the ground.

"I don't want to die," he said simply.

As the gun hit the ground Clint relaxed, and said, "I don't blame you, Varnes. Why did you hire Hedge and his partner to beat me up?" he asked.

"It wasn't nothing personal, believe me," Varnes said.

"Well, as soon as you explain it to me, I'll let you know whether I believe you or not."

"It wasn't my idea," Varnes said.

"Whose was it?"

"I was hired to hire them," Varnes said. "I was paid enough money so that I could pay them and still have some left over for myself."

"How much?"

"Fifty dollars each for them, and a hundred for me."

"That's not a lot of money, Varnes," Clint pointed out. "Was there another reason why you agreed to do this?"

"Uh, well, yes, there was," Varnes admitted.

"What was it?"

"What happens if I tell you?"

"You mean, if I believe you?"

"Yeah."

"I'm on my way back to Yankton," Clint said, "and you're on your way."

"Where?"

"Anywhere," the Gunsmith said, "as long as I never see you again."

THIRTY-SIX

As much as they pushed it to get to Bragg, Clint pushed it even harder to get back. He told Charlie that if he got too far behind he shouldn't push his horse to keep up.

"I'm in a hurry to get back, Charlie, but don't kill your animal trying to keep up."

"What did you find out?"

"Something I don't like," Clint said, "but I'm not going to say anything else until I find out more about it. I'll see you back in Yankton."

Clint got back to Yankton just before dark and put Duke up at the livery. Then he went looking for Marshal Hanks. A deputy was in the office and told him that he didn't know where the marshal was.

"What's your name?"

"Calvin Barnes, sir," the deputy replied.

"Well, Deputy Barnes, I'd appreciate it if you would

183

tell the marshal—when you see him—that I'd like to see him as soon as possible. It's very important."

"Yes, sir, I'll tell him."

Clint left the office and went to Yankton House, got a beer from the bar and walked to a corner table with it. He settled down, sipping the beer, and gradually became aware of the subject of conversation going on around him.

". . . happened all of a sudden. . ."

". . . thought it was gonna go on forever. . ."

". . . sure wasn't no surprise when they found him guilty. . ."

Clint sat straight up and listened for a few moments, then he left his beer standing on the table and walked out of the saloon. When he got outside he broke into a trot and headed for the office of the Yankton *Star*. When he reached it he found the door locked, but banged on it until Amy answered.

"Clint, what—"

"Amy, I just heard some talk in the saloon," he said, cutting her off. "Is it true? Did they come in with a verdict?"

"Yes, they did," she said. "Come inside."

She took his hands and pulled him into the office, then closed the door behind them.

"It happened all of a sudden, Clint," she said. "The jury went out and came back in fifty minutes."

"And the verdict?"

"No one was really surprised," she said. "They found McCall guilty of murdering Wild Bill Hickok." She took his hands and said, "He's guilty, Clint. He always was in your eyes, and now in the eyes of the law, too."

His heart was pounding as he realized that it was over. He almost felt dizzy.

"Are you all right, Clint?"

"Yeah," he told her. "I just feel like a tremendous weight has been lifted from my shoulders."

"Well, avenging Bill Hickok's death isn't up to you anymore," she told him.

"No, I guess it isn't," he said. "Was a date for sentencing set?"

"January third," she said.

"Then it's finished," Clint said. "They'll have to hang him."

He took a deep breath and let it out slowly. He felt different, somehow. He could get on with his life now. After he took care of one more thing.

"Do you know where the marshal is?" he asked Amy.

"Uncle Jeff? Not exactly, why?"

"He and I have to talk."

"What about?"

"I think he'll know the answer to that," he answered.

"What do you mean?"

"He's got some explaining to do."

"About what? Clint, what's going on?"

He hesitated, not sure he wanted to go into it with Amy until he talked to Marshal Hanks.

"That's what I'd like to find out," he said, "and your Uncle Jeff is the man who can tell me."

He started for the door and she said, "Wait—"

"We'll talk after I've spoken with the marshal, Amy," he said. "I promise."

She started to speak again, but by then he was out the door and gone.

THIRTY-SEVEN

Clint went back to the marshal's office, where he found Deputy Calvin Barnes still holding down the fort.

"Did the marshal come back yet?"

"Uh, no, not yet," Barnes answered.

"Well, I've got an idea, Deputy," Clint said, approaching the desk and the obviously nervous deputy. It was also obvious that the deputy knew who he was. "Why don't you go and find him for me, and I'll watch the office for you."

"I don't think I can—"

"Why not?"

"Well, we've got Jack McCall in a cell—"

"That's all right," Clint assured him. "I won't let him out."

"I don't know—"

"I do," Clint said. "Go."

187

The deputy hesitated, then stood up and said, "All right. I'll see if I can find him, but I'll be right back."

"I'll be here."

When the deputy left, Clint sat down at the marshal's desk and couldn't help but think about the fact that McCall, his friend's killer, was in a cell in the back. If he wanted to, he could go back there and...

But he didn't need to do that. It was all over. McCall had been convicted, and he would hang. That was all Clint ever really wanted. He decided to go in the back anyway, just to see McCall, maybe talk to him.

He stood up, thought about taking the keys with him, then thought it might be wise to keep the bars between them. He went into the cell block, and the only cell occupied was Jack McCall's.

"Hello, McCall," he said to the man lying on the cot.

McCall looked up at Clint, then recognized him from the last time he'd seen him there, and also the times he'd seen him in court.

"What do you want?" the scruffy little man asked.

"I just wanted to take a look at you, McCall," Clint said. "How does it feel to know that you're going to finally hang for shooting Hickok from behind?"

"Why don't you leave me alone?" McCall replied.

Clint stared at the little coward, and it disgusted him to know that this was the man who had killed Wild Bill Hickok.

"You know, I could come in there and take you apart, McCall," Clint said, "or I could just put a bullet through your brain from out here."

"Mister, I'm gonna hang," McCall said, "so why should I care what you do to me?" The little man lay back down on his cot and stared at the ceiling, an arm across his forehead. Clint stood there looking at him for a long moment, then turned and went back into the main office. As he was closing his door his back was to the front door and he heard the hammer on a gun cock.

"Just don't make any sudden moves, Adams," a voice said, and Clint obeyed.

"Are you going to shoot me in the back, Marshal?" Clint asked.

"I could have a few reasons to and get away with it," Hanks said.

"You think anyone would believe that you shot me while I was trying to help McCall escape?"

"No, but they might believe that I shot you while you were trying to kill him in his cell."

"Why would I do that?"

"To avenge your friend, Wild Bill Hickok."

"McCall is going to hang for that, Marshal. There's no point in me killing him."

"I don't think it's any secret how the death of Hickok has affected you, Adams. You haven't been thinking that straight—"

"I'm going to turn around, Marshal," Clint said. "Slowly. Don't get nervous."

"I've been a lawman a long time, Adams," Hanks said. "I didn't live this long being nervous."

Clint turned around and faced the lawman, who was holding his gun straight out in front of him, pointing at the Gunsmith.

"You didn't live this long making stupid mistakes, either," Clint said, "but you've made a few over the past few weeks. Don't make another one now."

"No mistake, Adams."

"Want to tell me what started it all off, Marshal?" Clint asked. "Was it you who shot at me that day in the alley?"

"It was me," he admitted.

"Trying to kill me, or trying to scare me off?"

"If I'd been trying to kill you, you would be dead," Marshal Hanks told Clint.

"When I didn't scare off you put the pressure on Varnes, paid him a few dollars to have somebody break into my room and beat on me. When that didn't work, you stopped trying for a while. What's it going to be now, Marshal?"

"You talked to Varnes, didn't you?"

"Yes, I did, in Bragg. He told me the whole story. Now I'd like you to tell me a story. What's this all about? What have you got against me?"

"Amy."

"Amy? What about her?"

"I don't like you hanging around her. She's too young for your kind, Adams."

"She's a grown woman, Hanks, able to take care of herself."

"That ain't true," Hanks said. "She needs looking after, and I've always been the one to do it. I looked after her whole family, and I'm still looking after her and her grandfather."

"Maybe it's time you stopped looking after other people's families, Marshal."

"Don't say that!" the lawman snapped.

Perspiration had popped out on the lawman's head, and his gunhand had started to tremble.

"Her family is my family," he went on. "It should have been my family. She should have been my grand-daughter."

"Hanks—"

"She's the image of her grandmother," Hanks said, ignoring Clint's attempt to speak, "the woman I should have married."

"She's not the woman you should have married, Hanks," Clint broke in. "Amy's not your granddaughter."

"I'm not going to let you use her, hurt her, and then leave town, Adams. I'm not going to let you do that."

"So you're going to kill me?"

"If that's the only way to keep you away from her."

"You're crazy, Hanks. The trial is over, McCall is guilty and I'm leaving town anyway, so don't give me that business about wanting me to leave. There's some other reason, one that's not quite natural."

"What are you talking about?"

"I don't think your feelings for Amy Walker stop at something paternal."

"What are you saying?"

"I'm saying that you were jealous because you thought she would end up in my bed, and then when she did, you went a little crazy."

"Jealous? I'm old enough to be her grandfather!" Hanks shouted, but the tears in his eyes belied his words. The old man was in love with the young girl, and he was crazed with jealousy because she'd been spending her time with Clint.

"You want to kill me, then go ahead," Clint said, "but I want to see you try to explain it to Amy afterward. See what she thinks of you then, Hanks. Go ahead, lawman, pull the trigger, get it over with."

Hanks flinched when Clint called him *lawman*, because he had been a lawman, and a good one, for many years, and what he was threatening to do now went against everything he ever stood for.

"Pull the trigger, *Marshal,*" Clint said.

Hanks stared at Clint over his outstretched gun, and the tears that had been forming in his eyes began to roll down his cheeks. He dropped his hand to his side, as if the gun had suddenly increased in weight, and then he dropped it to the floor. He shuffled, like an old man, over to the desk, took his badge from his shirt and dropped it on the desk top, and then turned and shuffled out the door.

Clint went to the desk and picked up the badge. He turned it over in his hands a few times, looking at it, then he dropped it on the desk and followed Hanks out.

THIRTY-EIGHT

"I don't understand," Amy said.

It was the next morning, and Clint had gone to see her before leaving town, to explain.

"He'd been taking care of your family for so long it just became too much for him. He never had a family of his own."

"He was always upholding the law," she said. "He was always a deputy or a sheriff and then marshal."

"A man gives up a lot when he takes up with the law," Clint told her. "The law is kind of like a woman who won't let go, but when she does, you fall hard. He needs your help now, Amy. I think you're going to have to look after him and your grandfather now. Can you do that?"

"I'll have to, won't I?" she said. "They're my family."

"Yeah," he agreed. "I guess they are."

"What are you going to do now?"

"I'm going to get on with my life," he said. "I wasted too much of it on the dead."

"I'm glad you realize that."

"Yeah, I realize a lot of things, now," he said. He leaned over and kissed her on the forehead. "'Bye, Amy. You've got a paper to get out with a big story."

He looked down at her headline, which read MCCALL GUILTY! He'd been waiting a long time to see that, and now it didn't seem to mean as much as he thought it would.

"Good-bye, Clint," she said, and he left the office.

He went over to the saloon, where he was supposed to meet Colorado Charlie Utter. Charlie was sitting at a table with two beers, and the Gunsmith went over to join him.

"When did you get in?"

"About an hour after you did," Charlie said, pushing a beer over to Clint's side of the table. "It's all over, I hear."

"Yeah," Clint said, picking up the mug, "it's all over."

"Will McCall hang?"

"No doubt about it."

"So that's it. What are you gonna do now?"

"I'll pick up my rig and just keep going," he added. "What about you?"

"I don't know," Charlie said. "I guess I'll just drift."

They finished their last drink together, and then Charlie said, "You look different."

"Do I?"

"Yeah, there's definitely something different about you today," Charlie said.

As a matter of fact, there was something different.

During the night, Clint had finally been able to dig deep inside of himself and bring out that unnamed "thing" that had been eating away at him, and examine it.

He felt better about things now, and it was time to move on.

"What is it?" Charlie asked.

"It doesn't matter, Charlie," Clint said. He finished his beer, stood up and put out his hand. "Thanks for everything, Charlie."

"Sure," Charlie said, shaking Clint's outstretched hand. "Take care of yourself, Clint."

"You too, amigo."

Clint went out in front of the saloon, where he had Duke saddled and waiting. He mounted up and said, "Let's go, big boy."

Riding out of Yankton, he thought back to the night before, in his hotel room, when he had been sitting in a chair by the window. It had been then that he sat back and reached down inside of himself and found out why he had started drinking when he heard about Bill's death.

He would have liked to think that it was because he and Bill were such good friends, but in truth that had been a small part of it. He had hidden the real reason away for a long time, and he took it out and looked at it.

It looked a lot like fear, which was something that Clint Adams was not used to looking at. When Bill was killed, and the fear came upon him, he had not been equipped to handle it, so he started drinking so he wouldn't have to.

Now it was almost all over. The man who had killed Hickok was going to pay. Maybe Varnes and Brady, or Charlie Rich, had put him up to it, that couldn't be proved, but McCall had pulled the trigger, and he was going to pay. That was it.

Except for identifying the fear, and he had done that last night. It had been relatively simple, once he figured it out, and it would have saved him a lot of grief if he'd been able to face it much earlier.

His very first thought upon learning that Hickok had been killed—from behind, by a coward's bullet—had been, *If it happened to Bill, it could happen to anyone . . . even me.*

He had taken a drink to wipe that thought out, and then another, and another.

He had always thought that he was prepared to die by a bullet, but maybe he hadn't been as prepared as he thought.

He hoped he was better prepared now, but still did not relish getting it from behind, like Bill. The one time that Wild Bill had gotten careless—for whatever reason—had cost him his life.

The Gunsmith would never let anything—fear, superstition, nothing—cause him to become that careless, ever. If he caught a bullet, he wanted it to be from the front, facing the man who fired it.

A better man.

That was the only way for Hickok, or a Gunsmith, to die.

Author's Note

On January 3, 1877, Jack McCall, the convicted killer of James Butler "Wild Bill" Hickok, was sentenced to be hanged on March 1.

The marker on the grave of Wild Bill Hickok reads:

WILD BILL
J. B. HICKOK
Killed by The Assassin
Jack McCall
Deadwood City
Black Hills
August 2, 1876
Pard, we will meet again in the happy
hunting grounds to part no more
Good Bye
Colorado Charlie
C. H. Utter

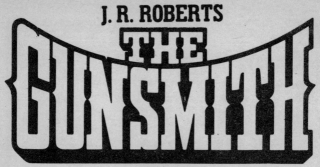